Dracula

Curse of the Castle

by
James Helms

DRACULA

DRACULA

To my wife and son, the two I cherish most

DRACULA

DRACULA

Table of Contents

Chapter 1: The Mall Walk..1
Chapter 2: The Passport Race...........................21
Chapter 3: The Library Visit..............................56
Chapter 4: The Wardrobe Chat.........................66
Chapter 5: The Flight..74
Chapter 6: Ride To the Castle..........................87
Chapter 7: The Tour...100
Chapter 8: The Bedroom Inspection..............114
Chapter 9: The Hallway Chat..........................141
Chapter 10: Six Room Split Up......................162
Chapter 11: Donnas' Struggle.........................176
Chapter 12: The Snack Attack.......................192
Chapter 13: Uncontrollable Emotions..........202
Chapter 14: Missing Mary................................214
Chapter 15: The Search for Mary.................229
Chapter 16: Bob's Investigation....................251
Chapter 17: The Room Transfer...................263
Chapter 18: New Ghosts Found.....................279
Chapter 19: Regroup..292
Chapter 20: Betrayal or Sacrifice.................301
Chapter 21: Fear vs. Love...............................320
Chapter 22: Ghosts Only Haunt At Night...339
Chapter 23: The Escape...................................349
Chapter 24: The Prize.......................................364

DRACULA

DRACULA

Chapter 1

The Mall Walk

This June, in Lansing, Michigan, there were eight friends who recently graduated from Eastern High School. They were eight close friends who make up a very low percentage of the graduating class. The eight friends have known each other ever since Kindergarten. Together they went to a local mall called the Meridian Mall.

With them now out of high school, their plans were to prepare for college. That is why they went to the mall. They thought that they could find outfits at the department stores that looked more professional than their high school wardrobes.

DRACULA

The mall was packed. With everyone out of school, the mall had traffic filling up nearly its entire parking lot. Just as packed as the parking lot was the mall itself. Stores were packed from one end of the mall to the other, and there was a big crowd rummaging through the malls passage ways.

In the malls passage ways, there were a number of kiosks trying to sell things, just as much as the stores try. At one of the kiosks stood alone a single salesman who did not have any items at his kiosk. All he had was a handful of pens and a huge stack of papers with a drop box. Everyone in the mall was passing by the kiosk with little to no interest. The group of teens who just got out of high school was headed towards the kiosk.

DRACULA

The group consisted of four boys and four girls. Each was only eighteen. Their names are; Bob Stevens, Frank Stein, David Wells, Mary Higgins, Janice Stokes, Alicia Fields, Arnold Cox, and Donna Steal. The eight of them have been looking through the mall for a while for new clothes for their wardrobes. To take a break, they saw that the kiosk they were headed to was not getting any business.

David, one of the boys in the group said, "How about we check out the kiosk there? It could be kind of cool to see what everyone else is passing by."

One of the girls in the group, Alicia was the first to say, "Okay. I think it could be interesting too."

The rest of them did not respond verbally, but they answered in their own way with a nod of their heads and a shrug of their shoulders. As they pulled themselves to the kiosk, the salesman noticed them, but did not say anything immediately. He had not been given any business all day and thought that this time was not any different. He saw people looking at their sign, but was not sure if they would be interested to hear what was going on at the kiosk.

The sign at the top of the kiosk read; *drawing for a trip to Dracula's Castle.* Each of them read the sign in an instant. Bob was the first to speak at the kiosk. He asked, "Sir, what is going on here? Why is nobody stopping here when the mall is packed?"

The man at the kiosk answered, "Well, most people I fear are fearful of the idea of going to Dracula's Castle.

DRACULA

According to legend, Dracula is an immortal vampire. Nobody seems to have the courage to see for themselves."

Donna replied with a sad voice, "It's seems pretty sad that nobody but us seems to have the courage to come and ask."

The man at the kiosk replied in a sad voice of his own, "Indeed. As people are afraid to come to the kiosk, I am getting bored by doing nothing all day." He took a short pause then said, "This kiosk is closing in two weeks than we do our drawing. So far, no one has entered."

Mary felt sorry for him. She thought it was not right that the kiosk was always getting passed by without any business to speak of. She thought it not right that this man spends hours working, and any potential customers just walk on by, as it was today until she and her friends stopped to ask questions. Feeling sorry for the man, Mary asked, "Why don't you explain everything to us? We know that it is a drawing to take a trip to Dracula's Castle. What else can you tell us?"

The man replied, "Very well." He then began to explain everything about the drawing, "There will be a drawing held in two weeks' time. There will be up to ten winners. The ten lucky winners will get a free trip, all expenses paid to go to Romania. They will spend one night in Dracula's Castle. Should they survive, they will win a prize of ten thousand dollars each."

David decided that he found this very interesting. He became curious of something though. Before

DRACULA

listening to another word he had to ask, "What happens if you don't survive in the castle for a full night?"

The man at the kiosk knew to expect this question. He had already planned to explain that part before being asked. He explained, "There are two ways to fail this dare, and only one way to win. The first way to lose is to leave the castle before sunrise the next day. The second way to fail is not to come out at all. Some who have gone there in the past they say have never been seen again. Either they ran away, never to be seen again anywhere near the castle, or they died inside, their bodies never to be found."

This was sounding more and more like a story they had seen before in horror movies and had read in horror books. This intrigued them even more. To live first hand a haunted house experience. What more could a horror buff ask for than to take part in the story?

In awe of what they had heard so far, the question had to be asked, and Donna decided that she would be the one to ask it. She began by raising the index finger on her right hand. This was known what seemed to be world-wide as a gesture meaning, just a moment. The man at the kiosk stopped what he was saying and let Donna speak. She asked, "If the bodies have never been found, and you think they never left the castle, than where could all those bodies be?"

It was obvious from her facial expression and the crackle in her voice that this concerned her a great deal. The man at the kiosk though did not know for sure the correct answer.

DRACULA

Since he never visited the castle himself, he had no first-hand knowledge on the subject. Although he was not certain, he knew it would be polite to try and give an answer the question asked. He tried his best by saying, "I do not know. It is possible since they were to have said to never be seen again. It is also possible that they were seen again, and lead full lives under a nom de plume. Which is correct? I cannot say for sure."

All of them were in awe. None of them could fathom what it would be like to live under a nom de plume. They were all happy with the names their parents had given them. Janice took a turn to reply to the man at the kiosk, and hos scary tale, "Sir," she began with hesitance. "How do we know if we will survive?" Still hesitant to learn more, she continued with a crackle in her voice, "I mean, if all those other people were never seen again, than how do we know that we will be seen again?"

Another question arose that the man at the kiosk did not have a true answer to give. With an honest look upon his face, the man did not know what else to say other than, "I have no guarantee. All I have are ballots for people to fill out. If I could, I would tell you that everything would be okay." He paused a moment then said, "But that would be a lie since I cannot predict the future."

Everyone understood. The man did not have any true answers, only empty ballots, a drop box, and his knowledge of the lore that surrounded the castle. The group of young teenagers would have to make their decision without a guarantee. The only thing that they knew for certain was that the drawing would end in two weeks, and that nobody had filled out a single ballot as of yet. It was almost a guarantee that they would all end up able to go, even if two more ballots were filled. The only thing that could stop them all from going was the possibility that three or more people would fill out other ballots. They knew that this was a possibility, but an unlikely one since nobody had filled out a ballot yet. Even on the busiest of days for the mall such as today, everyone else seemed to pass the kiosk with little to no interest.

Arnold held out his arms, waving his hands toward each other. He was giving the motion for everyone to huddle. None of them played

DRACULA

football, but they all knew how to huddle the same as football players do. As he motioned with his hands, Arnold also said, "Let's talk this over, just us."

Everyone went into a huddle. The man at the kiosk was still in ears reach. Once inside the huddle, the first to speak was Janice, "I'm not sure about this. With so many people disappearing, I am worried that we could end up disappearing too."

Everyone understood her concerns, for the rest of them heard the tale too and had the same concerns. Someone had to argue the other side though in order to weigh the pros and cons of filling out the ballots and accepting the possibility of going to a haunted castle, knowing that it was not just some ordinary castle, but rather the castle of

DRACULA

Dracula, the king of all the vampires, and one of the most feared names known to the modern world.

Knowing there must be two sides to an argument, the other side of the argument was coming from David, "While it is true that people in the past didn't make it, I think we need to consider that they went in alone. We are going to go in as an eight person group against one ghost, if that."

Thinking that they would have an eight to one advantage helped make their decision that much easier. Eight to one odds were much better than one to one odds which are what most people who visited the castle in the past more than likely had. Alicia continued the same argument as David began, "Just think, if two other people fill out ballots too, than we

DRACULA

could have ten to one odds, even better yet."

Donna now added her thoughts to the mix, "What if it is just us? Not one of us is a warrior. Why should we think we can beat a ghost who is an experienced killer?"

Arnold decided that it was his turn to inject his voice into the conversation, "What are the odds that there is a real ghost? I mean come on. We all know that haunts are just in horror stories. They aren't real."

After careful deliberation, the decision was made. The friends broke up their huddle. They separated in four sets of two. Two sets for each of the two sides of the kiosk. They decided to put their names into the drawing. David Wells and Alicia Fields was one set of two. Frank Stein and Janice Stokes were another set of two.

DRACULA

The four of them took one side of the kiosk. On the other side of the kiosk there stood the other two sets of friends. Bob Stevens and Mary Higgins was one of those two sets. The last and final set of friends, the ones who were on the same side of the kiosk as Bob Stevens and Mary Higgins were Arnold Cox and Donna Steal. Separately, yet still together they then took pen in hand and each filled out a form.

After filling out their forms, the man at the kiosk said to them, "Thank you. We will call those who win the drawing for the trip in two weeks when the drawing will take place."

After the man gave his thanks, they each nodded to say you're welcome without saying it aloud. Each of them wanted to say it, but they all knew that it would sound very repetitive. This is why the just nodded their response. The teenage group then continued on their way through the mall to continue their shopping.

As they were walking away, there was an uneasiness that settled in the pit of Donna's stomach. She was certain that it had something to do with the kiosk, or at least the man at the kiosk. She looked back, trying to find out what it was. She only looked back for a moment, and in that moment, she could not tell for sure what it was that was startling her.

In just a small distance away, there was something odd that nobody noticed while at the kiosk. It was too small to notice from a distance, and was hidden in the man from the

DRACULA

kiosk's eyes. It was kept hidden so well, that nobody could notice it unless actually searching for it. What was it that was hidden away so well? It was none other than the face of Dracula.

Two weeks had passed. Their shopping was done. As they waited to see if they would be getting the call for the trip prize they decided to find a way to pass the time. They went to a local park with a basketball court to hang out and pass the time playing sports. The boys played as the girls cheered them on.

During the game, they heard a phone ring. It was Arnold's phone. They were each hoping for a call, and it seemed calls would start taking place as they were shooting hoops. To answer the call, Arnold said, "Time out." He grabbed his phone from his shorts pocket. The phone number was not familiar. Still, he answered, hoping it was the call he had been waiting for. He hit the receive button on his phone, held it to his ear and answered, "Hello."

The person on the phone replied, "Hello." He then asked, "Is this Arnold Cox?"

"Speaking," replied Arnold.

The man on the phone said, "Hello Arnold. You recently filled out a form for a trip. You won the drawing as one of the people to visit Dracula's Castle, and stay there for one night."

Arnold could hardly contain himself. He was both excited that he won a spot in the drawing, and at the same time scared. The only words that he could say as he found himself in awe were, "Thank you."

DRACULA

The man on the phone replied, "You're welcome. You will receive your airline tickets in the mail soon. The trip will take place in three months. This will give you time to set up vacation time at work and so forth. Enjoy your trip."

The phone call ended. The others did not hear both parts of the conversation. They wanted to ask what the call was all about. What about the phone call put Arnold in awe? Before the question could be asked, another phone began to ring. The phone that rang next before the question could be asked was Donna's.

One by one, they each received their own phone call. Each call was the same, including the caller at the end of each phone call. Each was given a spot on the trip to Dracula's Castle. They were only slightly

DRACULA

surprised that they each got the call. They hoped that they would all be able to go, but they didn't know if anyone else would fill out forms. If anyone else did, it would be possible that they could take any of the eight spots they tried to get. They did not know if anyone else filled out a form. If anyone had though, it would have taken one of the last two spots available.

DRACULA

Chapter 2

The Passport Race

The eight high school graduates made a plan for the next day. After they each showered the next morning, they planned on meeting once again at their rendezvous point at the mall. The rendezvous point was at the food court, where they could sit down as they filled out the forms.

They did not all go to the mall straight from their homes though. Donna went from her house to the local Post Office to pick up eight forms to fill out in order to get their passports. After

DRACULA

Donna stopped by the Post Office she went to the rendezvous point to meet the others.

The other got to their rendezvous point only five minutes before Donna. As they waited for a moment, they found an area where they could all sit together. As she brought the forms, Donna said to the others, "Here we are. Eight forms to fill out."

As Donna passed the forms around, Frank took a turn to let his friends know of his contributions. "I thought we might need these," he said to everyone. Out of his pocket he pulled out in his hand eight pens. He had one pen for each of them to use. Frank passed out the pens to each of his friends. They all found the form straight forward and simple as they filled it out.

After they were done with the forms, they knew that pictures were going to be involved in the creation of a passport. They did not need the form to explain that photos were necessary. This they knew from all the passports they have seen in movies. The part that movies did not explain is that they needed the passport form to explain the questions in their heads such as, how many photos are needed per passport? What size do they need? With today being a high-tech world, are they supposed to be on a cd or memory card of some kind?

They learned that a plain background was needed. The pictures needed to be printed out. They required two copies of identical pictures. They learned that the size they needed was quite small, two inches by two inches. Knowing that pictures would be needed, Alicia brought her digital camera along.

Looking around, they saw a wall in the café where there were a few posters spread out against a white wall. Alicia, being the one who would be taking the photos said, "Here is perfect." She then gestured that they all get ready to line up one by one against the wall. She then continued, "Janice, you

DRACULA

first. I want to get all my lady crew in a row."

Slightly nervous, Janice stepped up to the wall and faced Alicia. As she finished flinging her hair behind her shoulder, Janice took a deep breath and exhaled. She then said to Alicia, "I'm ready."

Janice smiled. It did not look like a sincere smile though. Instead, it portrayed the look of someone posing instead of being themselves. Alicia took the picture anyway to keep as a memento. Afterward, Alicia informed Janice, "That was nice, but we are doing passport photos, not trying out for a modeling show." Then Alicia asked, "Can you give me a regular smile, without the posing?"

Janice did not give a verbal response that anyone could hear. Beneath her breath though, Janice said, "Okay." She then reset herself, and gave a new smile, one that looked more like a young woman who was happy as her picture was being taken.

Alicia took a picture of the new smile her friend was showing as a glow came over her face. As her picture was being taken though, nobody noticed that Janice had her eyes not fixated on the camera, but on Frank instead. How the marvelous picture came to be was not important to anyone. The only concern was

DRACULA

that the pictures got taken and printed to turn in their passport forms for processing.

After the second shot, Alicia said, "Much better, also much more believable. Nobody is a model at all times, not even models. Everyone needs to take a break at some point in time."

As she was finished, Janice walked away from the wall. She was pleased that her photo turned out so well, and on only the second try. Janice may not be now, but with her first photo, she was being considered as model material. Janice now thought of herself as model material. She thought of herself to be a model in the making, and Alicia as her exclusive photographer.

Alicia was ready to take her next photo. Donna was next in line as she was next to the wall when Janice was finished. Alicia saw her there and said, "Okay Donna, your turn."

Donna stepped into place against the wall. She then said after taking a breath to lessen the tension, "Ready."

With Donna now ready, Alicia got her camera ready. Just seconds before taking her shot, there was action going on behind Alicia. It was the guys along with Janice. They decided to make the photo taking more fun and they would make funny faces. Donna could not help giving a small laugh even though she tried holding it in until the photo was taken.

With the face making behind her, Alicia didn't notice it. With the photo not looking the best, Alicia said, "Donna, we need to go again. Your laughing distorted the shot and made it fuzzy."

Donna was both happy and sad about her picture needing to be retaken. She was happy because her friends made her laugh. She was sad because she had to redo the picture with the first one not coming out the best. Donna reset herself, clearing the laugh from her face while keeping a nice smile.

DRACULA

Again, the others tried to distract her with goofy looks. This time however, she was able to keep a straight face until the picture was taken. "The second picture," Alicia said, "turned out much better."

Alicia was already two down and one to go until the girls in the group besides her were finished. The last young lady to have her photo taken by Alicia was Mary. As Donna stepped back behind Alicia with the others, Mary stepped into place. She too took a breath before having her picture taken. Mary then claimed she was, "Ready."

Alicia was ready as well. Mary knew of the others making

goofy faces and was prepared for it. She gave a nice smile as Alicia took her first picture. This time Alicia said, "The photo was good. The first time was perfect. No retakes needed."

Mary was proud of herself for being the first one not needing a retake on her photo. Mary had a smile on her face still as she went behind Alicia to the others. As she headed back there, Mary said, "Awesome! One and done."

The guys knew that they were up next. In what order they were not sure. Before giving the guys a chance to elect what order to go in on their own, Alicia turned around and called, "Arnold, let's get started."

DRACULA

Arnold headed to the wall for his photo to be taken. On his way there, he said, "Let's get this done." He seemed determined to have his picture taken in one shot, not allowing anyone to distract him.

He posed for Alicia as she was getting ready to take his photo. The others on the back however, hiding behind Alicia, were still playing their pranks with making funny faces. Arnold thought it was funny when he was making funny faces, not so much now that they were being done to him. Just before Alicia took the photo of Arnold, he started to get mad at the funny faces his friends were making. Arnold ended up with a slightly mad face as the flash went off.

Alicia saw the photo on her camera's screen. She did not like what she saw. She knew that Arnold had a better disposition than that. Alicia decided to keep the photo, but at the same time she said in a suggestive voice, "Why don't we try that again? I think this photo wouldn't do you justice."

Alicia, as polite as she could be, knew how the last one turned out. She was hoping that there would not be a repeat performance when she went to take the next photo.

Arnold obliged as he said with disappointment in his tone, "Okay." He changed the look on his face, trying to get the nice looking young man look that Alicia saw, but was not yet being given as she tried to photograph him. Arnold finally put on a sincere smile. "Let's try that again," he said with the new sincere smile upon his face.

Alicia did not respond verbally. Instead, she gave a nod and got her camera ready to retake the picture before Arnold's expression changed again.

The others again played their pranks with funny faces to see if they could get Arnold for a second time. Alicia knew there had to be something bothering her friends, but was not sure what it was for certain.

DRACULA

Arnold knew what was going on, but he did not let Alicia in on the secret. With his friends taunting him, Arnold stood his ground this time. He kept the look on his face that he knew Alicia was looking for before she would dismiss him from the picture taking.

Alicia took her photo of Arnold for the second time. It looked much better than the first. Alicia had a smile on her face now, knowing that she was four down, and three to go. Afterwards another of their group would need to take her photo. Pleased with Arnold's second shot at his photo, and the smile on her face she said,

DRACULA

Now that's the Arnold I know. This one is a keeper."

As Arnold headed back to his friends on the other side of Alicia, Frank headed into position for his photo to be taken. Alicia did not call for the next person yet. Frank just showed up, as if to volunteer being the next in line to pose for one of Alicia's photos. As the two swapped places, Alicia noticed a grin on Franks face.

Frank was nowhere near camera shy. At the same time, Frank was not a poser. All of his pictures have always been natural. Keeping with the pattern on the other side of Alicia, hidden from her view was the rest of their group making funny faces yet

DRACULA

again. Frank was now the target of their clownish actions.

Alicia did not look back to see for certain what was making everyone needing to take retakes of their pictures. She did however have her gut instincts. She knew that there had to be a distraction of some kind to attempt breaking everyone's concentration.

Frank did his best to ignore the actions of the others, no matter how obnoxious they got. He did his best also to keep a natural look on his face. Frank was successful, where others before him failed. The others who were trying their best to be as silly as possible failed this test. Frank was a tough room. They thought to

DRACULA

themselves that they will need to be better next time.

While Frank made a good lasting impression on the others, Alicia took her shot, hoping that Frank would not give in before the shot was taken. Alicia was proud of herself when she took Frank's picture. She said as she took a look at it, "My best work as of yet, with Frank cooperating with me of course."

Frank went back to the others with a grin on his face. As he did, Bob approached the wall. He would be the next to test the others silly faces with his concentration. Bob had a less determined look on his face. Bob actually was slightly camera shy.

DRACULA

The idea of his friends taking his photo, or keeping a copy never bothered him. What was bothering Bob? Was it someone else seeing his photo, someone who he did not know? It was. Bob was not one to show his picture to everyone that was a stranger to him.

Alicia knew how Bob got when his picture would be shared with a lot of other people. He never looked forward to posing for picture day in school. Bob knew that picture would be shared with the entire school, and who knows how many countless others. This was the same. Instead of the photo being shared with the school body as a minimum, this time it would be shared with however

DRACULA

many people it took to create a passport. Strangers from different cities, different states, people who he had never met, nor ever will most likely.

Knowing how much all these things bothered Bob, Alicia knew she would need to be cunning, getting Bob to pose for her, and not be concerned about any strangers. Alicia had a plan in her head already, before Bob even approached the wall for his photo shot. Alicia decided that a distraction of her own making would be the best way to go.

Alicia decided that trickery of cunning would be an attempt to get Bob out of his head and make him blush, or at least give it a great attempt. Alicia asked with a soft whisper, making sure nobody else could hear, "Is Mary a good kisser?"

Bob was beside himself. He didn't know how to react to that. Was he to be embarrassed? Was he to be shocked? Was he to feel the urge to answer and reveal his own feelings possibly? Bob looked like he was deep in thought. He was trying to think of the best possible answer. Distracted, paying no attention to the camera, or his friend's foolish behavior Bob gave a smile.

Bob was in a day dream, a world all his own, locked away in his head. In his day dream, he thought of all the times he tried to

DRACULA

kiss Mary and failed. Someone or something was always preventing the connecting of their lips. Bob was also remembering the few times when he was able to pull off sneaking a kiss. Remembering those good times is what put that smile on Bob's face. It was a simple smile. It was not cheesy. Bob's smile was sincere. It was the perfect time for Alicia to get her shot in.

Alicia, remaining as quiet as possible put her camera into focus. As her flash went off, and her shot was taken, the flash of light snapped Bob out of his day dream state. Alicia saw the picture first and she remarked, "Good. Now,

DRACULA

all that's left for me to photograph is David."

The others tried so hard to distract Bob with their goofy facial expressions. What they did not count on was Alicia being able to pull off an even better distraction. With his photo now taken, Bob heads back to the others. He kept his smile the whole way back. Nobody could determine why he was still smiling.

Alicia did not see David approach the wall after Bob was leaving it. She knew he was the last of them that she could photograph. Since David was not heading to the wall on his own accord, Alicia said, "Come on David, you're up."

DRACULA

David heard Alicia. He sighed and then headed to the wall. On his way there, David said aloud, yet to himself under his breath, "Here goes nothing." David forgot for a moment that he was saying it as he was walking past Alicia, who, unknown to David heard him whisper.

Alicia waited for David to get himself into position. Once he was, Alicia responded to what David tried to keep whispered under his breath. First, Alicia got her camera ready; then, as she was making sure it was in focus she said to David, "No, here goes everything."

Their friends behind Alicia were once again making their

DRACULA

funny faces, doing what seemed to be their best. David was more puzzled than anything else though. His concentration was not focused on his friend's goofy behavior. Nor was it focused on Alicia's camera. David's focus was stuck in one place only, confused as to why Alicia said what she did. How did she hear me he thought to himself?

While David was still confused, Alicia took advantage of the situation. She snapped a shot of David with a confused look on his face. Proud of her sneaky shot that David was not prepared for, Alicia said, "That's a keeper."

David heard Alicia and realized what had happened. His being distracted opened up the opportunity for an unexpected snap shot. As soon as David realized what had happened he replied, "Hey! That was unfair. You cheated by distracting me."

Alicia knew that she still needed a better shot. She replied to what David just remarked by asking, "Are you ready to give me a good picture now? And stop paying attention to distractions?"

David knew that Alicia was right. If he concentrated on giving Alicia a genuine picture to take, and not be distracted by her talking, or their friend's silly faces, he would already be done with getting his picture taken correctly. David knew that he had done something wrong by not paying attention to the task at hand. Feeling silly himself, David gave a small chuckle and said, "Alright. Let's do this the right way."

David was embarrassed, which gave him all the more reason to give a genuine smile. He was laughing at himself on the inside. Seeing the look on David's face now is the look Alicia had been looking for all along. She took the picture straight away. She would not give David the opportunity to change his facial expression again before she took her shot. David's photo was much better the second time around.

Alicia was proud of what she had accomplished. She was able to get perfect shots of all her friends.

Most took two tries, but no matter if it took one attempt or multiple attempts, she got the job done. When her last shot was taken, and she was pleased with the results, with a sigh of relief Alicia said, "Finished."

David left the wall and approached Alicia. He gestured for her to give him the camera and said, "We're not done yet. We still have one more photo to take, yours."

Alicia knew David was right. She still needed to pose for her picture. She was just disappointed that she was not able to get everyone, including herself. Still, Alicia was satisfied with getting seven out of eight done by herself.

Alicia handed over the camera with a smile on her face. She knew that it would be best to let one of her friends take her picture rather than trying to take a picture of her own. Alicia sighed one last time and said, "Okay."

With the camera turned over and put in David's hands, Alicia headed to the wall for her picture to be taken, finishing up the last of eight photo's that was needed to be put in their passports. Alicia stood against the wall, waiting for her turn to be photographed. She now saw for herself what trickery her friends were playing behind her back. She saw the funny faces that most people couldn't help but to laugh at. Alicia chuckled when she saw the funny faces. She now saw with her own eyes and knew what turned out to be a big distraction for so many others.

David knew that the others were now playing their games with Alicia. Knowing this, David was already annoyed. He just wanted to get the final picture taken so they could go get them developed. In order to accomplish his goal, David rolled back his eyes and tilted back his head as if he were to look back at his friends behind him. He then said while in that position, "No more! Let's get Alicia's picture and get everything turned in."

The others were not quite certain what it was that was going

DRACULA

on. David had no problem in taking part in the goofy face distraction game with the others earlier. Why was his attitude different now? Was it due to the fact that he was now taking the last picture? Or could it be due to the fact that Alicia is his girlfriend and he wanted to be her knight in shining armor? They knew not which was correct, if either was.

Arnold spoke for the others by saying, "Dude, we're just goofing off like we've been doing all along."

David knew that Arnold was right. Why should they treat Alicia any different? They were all friends. They have all been having fun. Nothing had changed except who the photographer is. David regretted his decision of getting angry. He knew what the right thing to do was, so he said, "Sorry. I was just trying to finish up here."

Janice seemed to be more understanding. She knew they would have needed to take multiple doubles. She understood that David was just trying to finish what they started. She replied, "We know. Don't sweat it. Everyone gets to their breaking point. Maybe it was just too much goofing off."

David appreciated the gesture. He said to Janice feeling better, "Thanks. Now let's get that last picture."

DRACULA

Alicia was proud of David for standing up for her. She was also proud to call David her boyfriend. Seeing his courage to stand up for her in front of their friends was the most courageous thing Alicia had seen David do so far. It takes a big man to stand up for his girlfriend in front of a stranger. It takes double that to do the same thing in front of friends and family. Alicia loved David even more now. Her face was all a glow.

David saw the radiant glow coming from Alicia's face and knew; it was time to take Alicia's picture. David got the camera ready. He then snapped her picture before the glow disappeared. David said as he looked at the picture, "One and done. Alicia, you look good in every shot."

Alicia's face was still a glow. She had walked back to David to get her camera back and to see how her picture turned out. She wanted to see with her own two eyes.

David handed her back the camera and said, "Here. See for yourself."

Alicia took back hold of her camera. It turned out to be a better picture than she thought. She was surprised to see how well David had done taking her photo. As a reward for defending her, as well as getting her photo done

DRACULA

perfectly on the first try, Alicia said, "Thank you." Afterwards, Alicia gave David a kiss lightly on the lips.

With forms filled out and pictures taken, there are just two more chores to do. They all knew what those chores were. Frank however, was the one to mention it. "I will turn everything in on my way home after we get the pictures developed," Frank volunteered.

The others were delighted to see Frank step up and volunteer some of his spare time in finishing everything up. The most impressed was Janice. "That's my guy," she said with a smile upon her face.

DRACULA

Chapter 3

The Library Visit

With the forms taken care of, they decided to do some extra research to really know what they have just gotten themselves into. For the next week they took turns of whose house they hung out at and every night they watched a different Dracula movie.

David decided that what they hear in the movies was not enough. With each Dracula movie different in some way, he felt uncertain of the true Dracula story. Some of the movies tell of him being a ghost or a very old

DRACULA

man looking for a lost love. Others tell of him being able to transform into a bat; hence the name of a bat breed called the vampire bat.

Stories of Dracula also mention him as a prince who drank the blood of his enemies. It is said the reason he did so was to scare armies of other nations from coming to Romania in hopes to conquer it. Out of all the different stories, the main question came to be, "What about Dracula is truth, and what about Dracula is fiction?"

Even with that being quite possibly the biggest question, there was still yet another that loomed in the back of his head. It stayed there until he went to the library

DRACULA

to get answers. Once there he asked his question to the Librarian. His looming question was, "Excuse me, but do you have anything that can teach foreign languages, namely Romanian?"

The Librarian from the Capitol Area District Library responded in a form of multi-tasking. She answered, "One moment." Meanwhile, she types in the request with precision and speed. The Librarian got the answer practically immediately. She continued with her answer by saying, "It looks as though we have three different ones in stock. You can find them on the second floor in our language section."

DRACULA

With new information, David responded by saying, "Thank you." David then followed his instructions and proceeded to the second floor using the elevator.

The second floor is filled with only non-fiction material. When David got to the second floor he saw how not only was the non-fiction was taking up the entire floor, but he noticed how it had different sections. Nearly one half of the floor was taken up by one section, the reference section. It took a moment, but he finally noticed the sign for the language section. He walked over to the area and found not one, not two, but three different versions of Romanian-English dictionaries,

DRACULA

each with a different author. Not knowing what phrases or single words he would find to learn in each of the books, David did what he thought was best. He decided that the best thing he could do was to grab all three books to check out. One by one he grabbed them off the shelf and took them back to check out on the first floor.

There was a small line in front of him which took practically no time to clear. The lady at the checkout counter offered her assistance by asking, "Can I help you?"

David approached the counter with all three books in one hand. Due to each of them being small paperbacks, none of them took up much room in his hand. Together, when you see all three book spines together they were equivalent to one decently sized hardback novel. He laid the three books on the counter, much like a card player would show their winning hand, with the books fanned out. David then reached for his belt loop where his keys were located. Attached to one of the key rings was his miniature library card. He then said to the lady, "Here you are Ma'am."

The lady took his card to scan, keys still attached. She noticed immediately that all three books were on the same topic. With curiosity in her mind, she could not help but ask while scanning the books, "Are you taking a trip?"

David did not expect the amount of attentiveness as displayed by the lady. Not only was he surprised on how fast she caught on to the common link of the books, but he also noticed that she cracked a smile. As David caught on to these things he made a reply, "Yes. My friends and I won a prize trip to Romania." He then continued as he said, "I thought before the trip I would try to learn some of their language. You know, enough to get around while we are there."

Done with her scanning of the books and listening of his explanation, the lady handed him his books, along with a receipt and said, "Here you are. I hope you and your friends have a nice trip."

David noticed a sparkle in her eyes. He did not take it as a pass at him, but rather as the look someone gets when they are thinking of their fondest wishes. He believed that her wish was not to be confined behind a checkout counter of a library, but to go on an adventure. With that on his mind, and the thought of knowing all the names have been drawn, David did not want to shoot her hopes of travel any higher. He decided that no matter what kind of message he saw in her eyes he must end this through the use of common courtesy. Since she was

DRACULA

kind enough to check him out and wish him a nice trip, he decided to respond, "Thank you." David began walking to the end of the counter where he noticed plastic bags which were an option, not a must to use. On his way to the bags he paused and turned back to say, "Just so as you know, my friends and I won our trip through a name drawing at the mall. Who knows, it is possible you could be just as lucky."

With a new idea of how to fulfill her dreams, it seemed that the sparkle in her eyes sparkled even brighter now. Even though he did not mean to, David shot up her hopes to the moon. All he meant to do was to tell her that dreams can come true; you just have to be patient. It would always be possible for her to win the next drawing. Before he could accidentally boost anyone's hopes any further he finished his way to the end of the counter to grab a bag. Even though he was trying to get ready to depart, it did not stop the lady from saying, "Thank you."

David, pleased with his actions, said with his books bagged, getting ready to leave, "You're welcome."

Chapter 4

The Wardrobe Chat

Nearly the full two months went by just as fast as they came. There was only one week left out of the two months. On the same day, at nearly the same time all eight friends were returning to each of their homes after just finishing up their paper-work to sign up for their college courses. To the surprise of each of them they found something in the mail, something they have been waiting for impatiently. Each of them opened their mail for the day and what should they see inside of their envelopes they each received but their passports. Each of them breathed a sigh of relief knowing that with their passports now obtained they will be able to go on their trip for certain now. All that stands between them and the ten-thousand dollars each is an airplane ride and a one night stay in an old castle.

The last week was frantic. None of them thought to look up what style of clothes are in fashion halfway across the world. They each racked their brains and came up with ideas. Some of them came up with matching ideas, while others came up with new ideas to try out. They also wanted to see if they could come to a unanimous decision as to which idea sounded the best. Each of their minds was hard at work, thinking of ideas as they hung out at Mary's house. The girls were more concerned with fashion than the guys were.

Bob decided that he should speak his mind on this concern of fashion by asking, "You know what I think?" Before anyone had a chance to answer his question, which was rhetorical anyway he continued with his thoughts by saying, "I don't think it matters what is in fashion in Romania. Tourists dress in their own clothes and take pictures. They don't dress like people in other places. That kind of thing is for people in plays."

Luckily for Bob, he was at his girlfriend's house. One of the other girls may have dismissed him from their house, but Mary could never do that to Bob. No girl could ever make their own beating heart leave. Mary's heart unconditionally belonged to Bob, as his unconditionally belonged to Mary.

Mary was the only cool headed female in the bunch after what Bob said. Donna was the first to react on what Bob said however. She replied with anger in her voice, "You are a guy. Guys don't care as much about fashion as girls do. Girls always want to be in fashion."

Trying to keep an argument from escalating any further, Mary

DRACULA

decided to say, "You are both right okay! Guys are more laid back about fashion. If the guys want to wear what they feel comfortable in, that's no biggie. We girls can wear what we look comfortable in too, or what we think looks fashionable." She paused for a moment with a look on her face as though she just got a great idea. She then continued by saying, "What if we were able to find clothes that are both?" Before anyone had a chance to ask what she meant by that, she continued explaining her idea by saying, "You know we could find comfortable and fashionable outfits."

Everyone listened with the intent to find a way for the fights between themselves and a way to prepare fighting stories of myth or legend. Knowing where they were going, and what they have seen in the movies brought up a universal question in everyone's minds, "If we go to Dracula's Castle, what should we expect? Is he still in his castle? Is it haunted by his ghost? Is it haunted by the ghosts of the soldiers he killed in battle? Is it haunted by people who were castle servants when they were alive, hundreds of years ago?"

Janice decided she should get herself involved in the conversation by asking, "Guys, why don't you go home and pack some leisure clothes that you will be comfortable in?" She continued as she said, "In the mean time we ladies can decide what we want to look like for you during our first night in a castle, a possible enchanted castle. Who knows, you may enchant us there, or you may be surprised. We may find a way to enchant you."

With thoughts of what could happen in the privacy of a castle half way across the world, the guys could not help but get worked up. The idea that they could sweep their ladies off their feet in a castle like knights in the olden days stuck in their heads they could not help but come up with a multitude of ways to attempt flattering each of their beloveds in a castle like a knight. Arnold spoke up for the guys as to their thoughts without

DRACULA

giving away any of their ideas by saying, "We get it. You ladies want some time to decide want you want to wear during our trip. We will go so you can have your girl talk time."

The guys then began to head toward the door. As they headed out, David said, "See you later Alicia. I hope if you can't find comfortable clothes I might be able to find a way to fix that problem for you." David noticed as the guys were walking out the door that Alicia could not help but blush.

DRACULA

Chapter 5

The Flight

With the argument over, and the time of departure nearing, these eight souls get ready to depart. With their bags packed, and their flight taking off at 1:30 p.m., they plan to arrive early at 12:30. They hope this will give them the time they need to have them meet at the same spot, get their luggage on board and themselves seated. This being their first flight, together or separately they were not sure what to expect. No one among their group even

DRACULA

knew ahead of time if any of them got air sick or not.

Bob brought with him one extra item in his pocket as a health precaution. That item is crystallized ginger.

The first to arrive was Janice. Once there, she found a bench to sit at while waiting for her friends. Janice kept her eyes open for the others. The first person she noticed to arrive after herself was Donna. As soon as she noticed Donna, Janice waived her arms in the air and said, "Donna! Over here!"

It didn't take long for Donna to notice a voice shouting her name and waving arms in the same direction. She followed her friend's octopus like wavy arms and found it to be Janice on the other side of the crowd.

The others arrived one by one until they were all there. Since they had an agreed upon arrival time it did not take long until they were once again together. This time though was slightly different. It was the first time in the airport for any of them. None of them were able to take lead to show the others around for this reason.

You know what they say; sixteen eyes are eight times better than two. With sixteen eyes looking around for signs it took no time at all to find their way to their flight. One thing they

DRACULA

noticed was that they had two seats in each row for four rows straight. It was set up as two perfect rows of four from front to back one row being the guys and the other row being the girls. The only problem was that since they were mailed to them, and the mailer not knowing who was dating who, the couples were jumbled. The only way they could fix that was to swap the airline tickets around so each couple could sit together.

As everyone got aboard the plane reality set in. They knew that once they arrived in Romania they would need to stay the night in a castle they heard of for years in the movies. Questions popped

DRACULA

up in their minds. Like, "Is Dracula real? Or a horror story told many times over in many different ways? Is the castle haunted or is it just hype?"

Not knowing for sure they decided not to let fear rule their trip. Knowing it would not take long to get from Lansing to Detroit to change planes, along with curiosity running through their minds they could not fall asleep. The only thing they could do is sit there impatiently. They remained quiet so they could listen for any instructions on the plane. They were listening for, "Take off, and also landing. They noticed there were rules on the plane also, such as keep seat belt fastened."

DRACULA

Once they reached the Detroit airport they looked at the departure time to leave Detroit to get to the next stop on their way to Dracula's Castle. They noticed they had a five hour wait before their next plane was to take off. Alicia made a suggestion by saying, "It looks like we will be here through dinner time. Let's look around the airport to see what they have here to eat."

David, supporting his girlfriend said, "Okay, let's look around."

David was not the only one to support this idea; however he was the only one to do so verbally. The others nodded their heads and began looking for signs that would lead to a restaurant at the airport.

After finding a bite to eat and finding their way to the terminal to their next plane they found themselves securely aboard taking a long flight from Detroit to Amsterdam, Netherlands.

They knew this plane ride would take the longest so they took the opportunity to get a nap, or at least try. They each had thoughts racing through their minds. What will they find at Dracula's Castle? Who will they find in Dracula's Castle? How much longer until they get there? These and many more questions are racing through the minds of all eight friends. One other thought in their minds is that they should all get some sleep so they are not so bored during a long flight.

Some of our friends found it easier than others to put these thoughts on the back burner and fall asleep. The ones that took slightly longer were Bob, Donna and Janice. They too were able to go to sleep. While the others were able to fall asleep almost instantly, these three did some tossing and turning, at least what they could of it while stuck in an airplane seat.

The excitement that they placed in the back of their minds did not want to stay there long, nor did it let them nap all the way to Amsterdam, Netherlands. They

DRACULA

woke up only thirty minutes before landing. This gave them time to try to stretch while sitting down. To break the ice from hours of silence while napping, David asked, "Alicia, how are you feeling about this trip?" He continued as he said, "We are almost there."

Alicia responded, "You're right. We are almost there. All that is left is one last plane hop and we will be in Romania." Realizing she hadn't answered her beau's question she continued, "And I feel excited. This will be our first time not to have our parents watching over our shoulders." She then had a thought and decided to share it with David, "Maybe if we are as alone as I hope, maybe for once we can act out how we feel without Sunday school rules in the back of our heads."

David caught on rather easily. He replied with a grin on his face, "I don't think they had four rooms in mind. Since the offer was for ten people they probably had ten rooms in mind. They had no way to know if couples would win the drawing together or not." Then he revealed the reason for the grin to Alicia, "That does not mean we can't find a way to go to each-others rooms or even share a room completely."

The wheels in the heads of all eight friends then began to turn more rapid than ever. It became a

DRACULA

race in each friend's subconscious, a race to see who would come up with the best story of how to get each couple in rooms together. Before they had much time to think about it the plane was landing and their thought race had to take a back seat while they dealt with the exiting procedures of the plane.

Being so close, they made good time while they boarded their last plane. This one took them from Amsterdam, Netherlands to Bucharest, Romania. It was a short flight from the Netherlands to get them to the capitol of Romania.

As they exited their final plane, Arnold was the first to

notice a man holding a sign written in English. He pointed it out to his friends and said, "Hey guys look. There's a sign over there in English. I think it's for us." It reads, American Prize Winners This Way.

Everyone began to get knots in their stomachs. They realized how close they were, and they finally realized the uneasiness of going to a place that was thought to be haunted. Now that they were in Romania, there was no going back. All they could do was push on. They only needed to stay one night. That shouldn't be too hard they thought.

They were all excited to have an escort to the castle. The one

DRACULA

that expressed it the most was Frank as he said, "Yes! We don't need to worry about no cab, no nothing. Way cool!"

Janice thought that it was cool too. She commented, "Let's go. If that sign is for us, all we need to do is go for a ride."

DRACULA

Chapter 6

Ride To the Castle

The friends headed over to the man holding the prize winners sign. The first to say anything to this man was Mary. With excitement from her hopes if being treated like a princess she said to the man, "Hello! We are the American prize winners!"

Unfortunately the man was not fluent in American English, not even from eccentric young ladies and having no idea why she was acting this way. The man responded in Romanian, "Cum vă pot ajuta?"

DRACULA

Mary asked, "What did he say?"

David then stepped in and said, "Yeah, I studied Romanian over the summer just in case." He continued as he explains, "The man asked, "How can I help you?" David then said, "Maybe I should talk to him." He then directed his speaking to the man and said in Romanian, "Da. ca câştigătorii American. Sunteţi noastre demnitarilor la Castelul lui Dracula?"

The man responded, "Da. Vă rugăm să urmaţi-mă." The man then moved his right hand to indicate which direction he wanted them to go.

DRACULA

Mary, being the one who wanted to talk to the man asked David as they followed the man, "What did you two say to each other?"

David explained once again, this time to his friends, "It was simple. I told him," He then repeated what he said in Romanian again, this time in English. He explained, "I told him; yes. We are the American prize winners. Are you our ride to Dracula's Castle?" Unfortunately David knew his translation was not complete yet. David had yet to explain the man's response. He continued by saying, "Then he told me," David then quoted the man in English and said, "Yes. Please

DRACULA

follow me." David finished his long explanation by saying, "And here we are following him just as he asked us to."

Now that Mary got her translation explanation she seemed satisfied. Mary was at a loss for words with her head hurting from trying to understand Romanian accept to say with a clueless look on her face, "Oh, okay, if you say so."

Alicia on the other hand knew she herself could not translate any Romanian talk, but her beau could. She had a grin on her face from ear to ear. While holding David's hand on the way out to the car with her free hand she said, "That's my man." She

DRACULA

then tried to be sneaky and gave David a kiss on his cheek.

David saw it coming but pretended he didn't see anything. David took the kiss as is, a reward for studying Romanian to help himself, and his friends on this trip.

Once they got to the car they noticed it was no ordinary car. It was a car big enough for at least ten passengers, a limo. The man opened the back door for his eight passengers and said in Romanian, "Vă rugăm să introduceți."

Alicia took a turn to ask, "What did he say?"

David found it amusing that no one understood the man this

time since he was kind enough to open the door for them. He laughed for a moment and said, "He just said," he then quoted the man once again, "Please, enter."

Alicia had to laugh at herself, for asking a question with such an obvious answer. One by one they entered the limo. Once they were all in the man closed the door and began to drive.

The friends all realized they had a chance to see parts of a foreign country with a guide from the airport to Dracula's Castle. Janice decided to electronically roll down the windows. Frank then asked her, "Hey sweetie, what are you doing?"

DRACULA

Janice found the question silly. She responded with a question of her own, "What do you think?" Before frank or anyone else had a chance to respond, Janice answered her own question as well as Franks. Her answer was, "I am lowering the windows, duh. I thought it would give us a better view so we can see more of Romania on our way to the castle."

Arnold decided to add in his thoughts by saying, "Good idea Janice."

For the remainder of the ride they remained quiet as they looked out the windows to try and locate attractions along the way. All of the sudden, the limo stopped

DRACULA

about a block away from the castle entrance. Frank asked, "I wonder what happened?"

David answered, "I don't know, but I'll go check with the driver." David then exited the limo and noticed that the driver had already exited as well. David walked up to the driver and asked in Romanian, "De ce opri?" David chose to ask his question in Romanian knowing the driver didn't speak English.

The driver responded in Romanian, "Eu sunt prea frică să conducă la castel. Sunteți pe cont propriu pentru a obține restul de drumul spre Castelul lui Dracula."

DRACULA

David asked in Romanian then, "Cât de departe suntem încă?"

"Doar despre un singur bloc" the driver answered in Romanian.

David responded, "Ok, vă mulțumesc pentru a lua acest lucru ne de departe." He then went back to the limo to inform his friends. He explained, "I saw the driver outside the limo and I asked him, "Why did we stop?" David continued as he said, "Then the driver said to me, and I quote: I'm too afraid to drive to the castle. You are on your own to get the rest of the way to Dracula's Castle." David continued as he said, "I then asked, "How far away are we still?" David explained,

"The driver told me about one block." David continued by saying, "Then I said to him, okay, thanks for getting us this far." He ended his story of what happened by saying, "And here we are, about one block away from the castle entrance."

Bob then replied, "I guess it's on foot from here, but one block isn't too far."

One by one they exited the limo and grabbed their luggage. The luggage was light considering it was only a one night stay. Once everyone had grabbed their luggage David said, "Follow me." He then pointed in the direction of the castle and said, "One more block this way to the ten-thousand dollar cash prize."

As they exited, they did not know why a driver would be so worried. After all, it wasn't the driver who would be staying the night in the castle. They did however pity the driver. To live and work so close to the castle, and yet choose to remain so far away, it seemed to them that it could not make sense. If one is scared of something, they can either choose to face it head on, or run and hide. One thing was for certain though; one block did not take too long to walk though. It merely seemed unnecessary.

Before they knew it they were almost to the door. As they

approached the door they noticed a pair of guards by the entrance. Each guard was panic stricken as they grasped their HOLY BIBLE as a policeman would grab their gun. It is looked at as the only means of protection by them as they look to protect their souls from what lies within the castle walls.

Unbeknown to them, they were being watched by a pair of eyes coming from the tower. Once they reached the door, they noticed no rope to pull on, nor a door bell of any other kind. The only way they saw available to let the caretaker of the castle know they were there was to grab old fashioned door knockers designed after gargoyles. Bob gulped and

DRACULA

said, "I will knock to see if anyone is here." Bob used the knocker to knock three times.

DRACULA

Chapter 7

The Tour

After knocking, they waited for someone to answer the door. It did not take more than a minute and the door crept open with a squeaky sound. The caretaker answered the door, knowing some English. He said, "Hello, you must be the American prize winners." He then extended his arm toward the inside of the castle. He continued as he said, "Please, enter. Let me show you to your rooms."

Janice seemed flattered by his polite manners. One by one

they entered and waited just inside the door, waiting for the door to be closed and the caretaker to lead them to their rooms. Janice said, "You seem so fluent in English for someone who normally speaks Romanian. It is quite impressive."

The caretaker found the compliment somewhat flattering. Now with everyone inside he said, "Follow me." The caretaker then grabbed a lit torch to see his way through the castle and to lead his guests through the castle as well. He then turned down a long hallway with lots of doors. Everyone noticed a spiral stairway next to the long hallway. The caretaker did not mention it in any way, nor did any of his guests ask about it. He opened the first door and said, "This is the common room. It is similar to what you call a living room."

Everyone took a turn to look inside the room. It was furnished with sofas and chairs with both incredible comfort and support. Along the wall across from the door was a montage of books on shelves reaching nearly to the ceiling. Along the side of the book shelves stood huge stone pillars, pillars that once held gargoyles for decoration in a time now past. You could see some remains of the gargoyles still remaining. Its furnishings were to awe over. It was noticed quite easily that no electronics were in the room, nor were there any between the room and the front door.

Once everyone had a chance to see the room the caretaker motioned across the hallway with his torch to a room with a door nearly parallel to that of the common room. He then led his guests to the door in which he motioned at and opened it. He then said, "This is the lavatory." He paused a moment then continued, "Better known to you young folk simply as the bathroom."

The lavatory is one room no one felt like examining. The caretaker then led his group of guests to the next door down on the same side of the hallway. He opened the door and said, "This is the kitchen. It has a pantry in the back. You will however have to cook things in older ways, ways used before electrical appliances were invented."

Hearing that news made everyone think the food selection was slim to none. Without looking, everyone assumed it was things that did not need either heating or refrigeration. Once again, leading his guests across the hallway was the caretaker to a door nearly parallel to that of the kitchen. He opened it and said, "This is the dining room."

Everyone took a turn looking in the room. It had a long banquet style table covered with a fancy table cloth held down with the use of the candelabra. They saw one on each end and one more in the center. The caretaker used the candelabra as a fancy candlestick decoration in the dining room. It has a single stand with a three claw design to stand it up properly on the table. The top branches off with four arms to each hold a candle. There was also a candle sticking up from the very center. They were black with blood red candles. The stands have a thorn design in the main stand piece and arms. They resemble black stemmed rose bushes with the blood red candles as the top piece as though they were black stemmed red roses.

To add to the lighting of the room, there was also a candle lit chandelier hanging from over the table. The table had many chairs surrounding it with one on each end. The table and chairs were a matched set. The chandelier was old and rustic. It seemed as though the chandelier was the original lighting tool of the room. It almost seemed to be out of sorts with updated furniture. Although the table and chair set was much newer, the caretaker made sure to get a set that looked old fashioned to resemble what was used back in the fourteenth century. The room's rustic beauty was to awe over.

DRACULA

Seeing the splendor of the dining room, and appreciating its rustic beauty, Donna said before leaving the room, "This room is amazing. It has a certain rustic beauty to it. I wish my house had as beautiful a design. It looks like something out of a fairytale."

The others appreciated the beauty of the castle too. To make Donna feel like she was not alone, Arnold said, "I agree. The place has a certain look to it. A classical look that seemed or seems to have been forgotten over the years. It is nice to know that not everyone has forgotten it."

The friends were feeling much better after seeing the hallway and four rooms and not a ghost to be seen. The friends also knew that soon they would be coming up to the bedrooms and had plans of their own with the bedroom arrangements.

Once everyone has had a chance to look over the dining room, the caretaker took the lead to the next room down along the same side of the hallway as the dining room. The caretaker opened the door and said, "This is the first of ten bedrooms along this hallway. There are five along this side of the hallway, and five along the other side." The caretaker then looked at a list he had in his hand and said, "This room is bedroom one, assigned to Bob Stevens."

DRACULA

The caretaker continued on as he crossed the hallway to the door almost directly across from Bob's room. Much to the caretaker's surprise, Bob stayed with his friends to find out who got assigned to each remaining bedroom. Nobody noticed, but when the door to Bob's room was opened, the only thing in sight, bedroom furniture was not the only thing in the room. Once at the door to the next bedroom, the caretaker opened it. He then said, "This is bedroom two, and has been assigned to Donna Steal."

Donna followed Bob's lead. She too chose to stay with the group after learning where her room is. The caretaker was less surprised the second time around. Just as Bob's room, nobody noticed anything in the room other than bedroom furniture. There were hidden things in Donna's room as well.

The caretaker then kept one pattern, while abandoning another. The next bedroom the caretaker stopped at along the hallway was on the same side of the hallway as that of Donna. The caretaker opened the bedroom door just as the others and said to his guests, "This is bedroom four. It has been assigned to Janice Stokes."

The first thing that entered everyone's minds was, "I thought this guy could count." Of course to be polite to their elder, none of them said it aloud. Janice took a moment to examine her room too. She then kept the pattern going with staying with her friends. What none of them realized right away was a pattern with odd numbers on one side, and even numbers on the opposite.

The pattern of the friends all taking the tour continued as well. None of them notice anything out of the ordinary in any of the rooms. Bedroom three turned out to be assigned to Arnold Cox. Bedroom five was then assigned to Frank Stein. Mary Higgins was assigned to room six. She was followed by Alicia Fields being assigned to room eight. Last but not least, David Wells was assigned

DRACULA

to room seven. With all of his guests shown to their rooms, the caretaker was ready to depart and let them attempt their challenge. Before letting him go though, Mary decided to ask, "Excuse me, but what about these last two rooms?"

The caretaker responded, "Those rooms were to be charged to two other guests. We were expecting ten. But only you eight showed." He continued as he explained, "These last two rooms were made for expected guests too. I suppose if any of you find your assigned rooms not to your satisfaction, you may take one of the last two remaining bedrooms." The caretaker ended what he had to say by saying, "Good night. I

DRACULA

hope all goes well tonight." With that he finished his departure from his group of guests and exited the castle for the night.

The friends were now alone. It was now up to them to make themselves comfortable for the remainder of the night. As the castle was departed by the caretaker, the guards remained. There was a full moon which was now high in the sky. It was now dusk. Their challenge was to remain there 'til dawn.

DRACULA

Chapter 8

The Bedroom Inspection

One by one, with the caretaker no longer being their guide the friends separated and went to their rooms. As they separated, Bob said to everyone attempting to make small talk, "I guess it's time to check out our rooms for the night."

Everyone agreed that it would be nice to see what kind of condition each of their rooms are in, at least more than what a quick glance can tell you. Mary

DRACULA

could not help but think there are more things that she would like to check out, more than she could see in her room at first glance. She was not shy in the least to let Bob know what she was thinking as she said, "I would like to check out more than just our rooms for the night."

"Me too," replied Donna. "It's not every day you get to check out an old castle without being told where to go, and when you could go there."

With that, they went to their rooms in order to unpack and unwind. David and Alicia entered their rooms first being closest to their bedroom doors. It did not take long for the others to *get back to their bedroom doors, enter their rooms and relax on their beds. David set his luggage down beside his bed and decided to lie down for a moment before unpacking.*

Alicia had the same idea. She laid her luggage bag beside her bed. As she began to sit down she saw something. It was transparent and near her bedroom window. It was a female ghost looking out the window. The ghost was acting harmless, but the thought of seeing a ghost was overwhelming to Alicia. She froze for a moment in fear. Once the paralysis of fear wore off, she ran to her door.

At the same time, David saw a ghost soldier in his room. It stood in a proper soldier position as if he were saluting a superior officer. David was beside himself. Not only did he not believe in ghosts, but he never expected to see an apparition of any kind in his life time. David did not know what to expect. He could only hope the ghost was friendly.

Before David could comprehend what would happen next, the soldier spoke. He said to David in Romanian, "Bună ziua acolo străin. Am fost prins în Castelul de sute de ani. Putea să mă ajute rupe acest blestem?"

Since David studied Romanian, he knew that the ghost soldier said, "Hello there stranger. I have been trapped in this castle

DRACULA

for hundreds of years. Could you help me break this curse?"

David was no longer afraid of the ghost in his room. He even used the Romanian he studied to talk to the ghost. David had questions that he hoped the ghost could answer. The first and most important question David could think of was, "Cum pot rupe blestemul pe Castelul?" David asked this in Romanian, as to make sure the ghost understood him.

David knew what he was asking. "How can I break the curse on the Castle?" Their conversation continued as David decided to unpack simultaneously.

DRACULA

Meanwhile, Mary and Frank were the next ones to inspect their rooms. Neither Mary, nor Frank noticed anything out of the ordinary as they entered their rooms. They each followed the pattern of deciding to lay their luggage bags each next to their beds.

Shortly after setting down her luggage and sitting down, Mary began to notice noise coming from the closet in her room. It sounded like a heated argument, but she was not sure what was being said. So Mary decided to inspect the possibility that someone snuck into her room and was trying to hide in her closet. She slowly walked toward her closet and in a feared voice asked, "Who's there?"

What she did not know, was that in her closet, there stood two ghosts in torn armor with blood on the armor. One of them was a soldier from the Romanian army from hundreds of years ago. He was a soldier who served under Dracula during his reign of the Romanian empire. The other was a soldier from another army during the same time period. His army tried to conquer Romania and was defeated by Dracula and the Romanian army. He too wore armor and had blood all over which seemed to stem from his neck.

DRACULA

To this day, the two soldiers' cannot see eye to eye. In life they fought for their respected armies. In death they argue over whether the curse set on Dracula's castle should be lifted or not. The Romanian Soldier said in his native tongue, "Îmi place fiind în măsură să rămână pe pământ!" When Mary heard the ghost, she did not know was that what the soldier said. Mary heard an argument in a foreign language. She did not know that what he ghost said was, "I love being able to stay on Earth!"

  The response of his enemy in life, and constant debater in death said in an argumentative tone using Romanian, "Mi-ar mult mai degrabă să fie pace în cer. Numai în cazul în care acest blestem ar fi plecat. Spiritul meu are nevoie de odihnă după sute de ani a fost prins în această blestemat castel." Once again, Mary did not recognize what was being said. She did not know that what was said this time was, "I would much rather be at peace in Heaven. If only this curse would be gone. My spirit needs rest after hundreds of years of being trapped in this cursed castle."

Mary did not know for certain what was being said. Nor did she realize right away that it was ghosts she peaked arguing in the closet. Mary then saw two ghosts arguing in a foreign language, both wearing armor, and both covered in blood. The ghosts paid no attention to her as their argument was the only thing on their minds as it has been for hundreds of years now. Frightened out of her mind, Mary felt like screaming but fear seemed to have robbed Mary temporarily of her voice. Finding that she was feeling voiceless, Mary decided to slowly back away, hoping not to be noticed. As soon as she was out of view she ran toward her door.

Frank's luck was not much better. He too tried to relax on his bed. Before he sat down though he noticed the sheets looked a bit lumpy. Frank thought nothing of it as he figured that maybe they arrived before all the bedrooms were attended to. Frank decided to make the bed the way he normally makes it at home. As he pulled the sheets back in an attempt to straighten them out he saw a female ghost asleep in the bed.

She was wearing a night gown that was stained with blood around the neck and shoulder area. She looked as if she had bled out and became unconscious from blood loss. This ghost, who now looked asleep in bed, could at last rest for an eternity. She stayed resting in bed, just like the other ghosts, her soul to never pass on.

Frank also noticed the source of the blood on her came from a cut in her neck. Frank was not sure what to make of this. He found many thoughts race through his mind. Questions accumulated in his mind faster than the answers he concocted in order to explain away the sight before him. Some of the questions that entered his mind that he could not seem to find answers to were, "Why is there a ghost in my bed? Why is the ghost asleep? I see blood on her neck and clothes, where is the rest of the blood? Was the rest of the blood absorbed into the mattress? Is this the mattress she died sleeping on? Will I die if I sleep on this mattress too?" These and many other questions entered his mind. The overload between

DRACULA

fear and curiosity scared Frank out of his wits. He dropped the sheets back over the ghost and ran toward his door.

Next to enter their rooms were Janice and Arnold. When Janice entered her room she was in awe. She thought it was so beautiful; it had to be the bedroom once used by a princess. She began to look at every piece of detail. She noticed everything from the marble floor to the linen used to decorate the window, headboard and footboard on the bed. It was like a bedroom she dreamed of as a child when she played pretend, being a princess. She thought the room was too beautiful to ever leave. She dreamed of staying in this room for not just one measly night, but 'til the end of time. That was, until she noticed the one fatal flaw in the room's artistic beauty.

As Janice ran to the window to see if the view was as magnificent as she had hoped she threw her luggage toward her bed. She opened the curtain and much to her chagrin she noticed the bedrooms fatal flaw. It was a male ghost wearing what looked to be beggar clothes from hundreds of years ago, hanging by a noose just outside her window.

The ghost was facing toward the window looking inside Janice's room. As the ghost saw Janice through the window he said, "Lasă acest loc! Feriți-vă blestemul acest castel este însoțită de!" Janice was unaware at the time that what the ghost said was, "Leave this place! Beware the curse this castle is accompanied by!" Not only did Janice not understand Romanian, but to go with it, it was next to impossible to hear the ghost through the window.

Not knowing the ghost was only trying to give her a friendly warning; Janice saw what her eyes would let her see. She saw a ghost hanging by a noose outside her window talking to her in a language she did not understand. She thought the ghost was trying to scare her, not warn her.

DRACULA

Janice became petrified. If there was an actual ghost outside her window, who knows how many more are somewhere in her room. Janice quickly let go of the curtain and ran toward her door in hopes of running directly into the arms of her beau, Frank.

Janice screamed the entire way from her window to her door. By the time she got to her door she was still scared, but somewhat comforted by the thought that she would soon be in Frank's arms.

Arnold on the other hand noticed a noise as he entered his room. The noise came from a swinging chandelier on the ceiling. Arnold thought it was nothing more than the wind blowing the chandelier as he refused to see for himself what the true cause was. Arnold sat his luggage beside his bed and walked toward his window looking to perhaps close it and therefore stop the draft that was moving the chandelier in his room. Now, when he got there he noticed that his window was closed, and therefore could not be the cause of why the chandeliers moving.

Not noticing any other place a draft could enter his room, he hesitantly looked up toward the chandelier. He was in awe at the site he was to behold. He thought either his eyes were deceiving him, or he was watching the best magic trick he ever saw. It was a male ghost with a slit throat swinging on the chandelier. The only reason Arnold could conceive as to why the ghost said nothing was that the ghost could not speak in death as he could not speak at the end of his life with a slit throat.

Such an idea was so appalling to Arnold, he dreaded even thinking it. Like the ghost, Arnold could say nothing. It was not as though his throat was cut, but rather seeing the results of such a massacre rendered his voice silent for the moment. Arnold wished to yell and ask his friends for some form of comfort that what he saw was not to be repeated to him. Instead, he could do nothing more than breath though.

It was similar to witnessing an asthma patient without their inhaler, gasping for every little breath, trying to stay alive. Lucky for Arnold, he had no such illness. It was but shock and fear that drove him to a breathless moment. As soon as the initial shock wore off he was able to breathe normally once more, but his voice did not return so promptly.

Arnold ran toward his door, wishing to yell at the top of his lungs but with no sound exiting his mouth. Only air passed through the passage way used by air, sound, food and drink.

Last but not least, Donna and Bob entered their rooms. Donna thought her room was very rustic. She appreciated the rustic design and felt as though she went back in time a thousand years. The beauty of the past brought to life in the present was something to awe.

Looking at the rustic charm of the room, Donna did not notice anything out of the ordinary as she sat her luggage down beside her bed without actually looking where she set it at. She could not take her eyes off the design of the room. Donna looked at the walls, the ceiling and even the closet.

Against the wall near her bed she noticed a wardrobe. It

DRACULA

was made with old-fashioned wood and had side-by-side doors that opened from the center out to the sides. As soon as it was seen by Donna she said to herself, "Oh!" As soon as the initial shock to see such beauty wore off, she flew over to it, hoping to see a beautiful princess dress inside. Donna was slightly winded when she got to it but did not wait to catch her breath as she flung the doors open. Donna found herself with no time to catch her breath as she began to scream.

Donna saw within the wardrobe a female ghost that made her feel sick to her stomach. Just the sight of the ghost made her scream. She had fear of

DRACULA

ending up the same as the ghost. The ghost's mouth was sewn shut. Her body was tied to the back of the wardrobe by rope. She had torn clothes from head to toe with patches of blood all over. The female ghost kept her eyes closed at all times even though they were not sewn shut like her mouth. What was not realized by Donna was the reason she kept her eyes closed. Before death, hundreds of years ago her eyes were ripped from their sockets.

As soon as the loud scream ended, Donna slowly closed the doors of the wardrobe hoping not to upset the ghost inside. As soon as she felt the ghost was not trying

DRACULA

to chase her, Donna ran for the door as quick as lightning.

Meanwhile, Bob examined his room. Trying to act sporty he slid his luggage across the floor attempting to get it by the bed. As he let go of his bag he declared, "Eight ball in the corner pocket." With his hands free, Bob rubbed his hands together and saying his thoughts out loud as he said, "Time to explore."

Being curious of what is in his room Bob conducted his own search of his room. He wanted to know what was there. Are there any games to play? Curiosity had him search all over. He went over to his bed and instead of getting on the bed he got in the push-up

DRACULA

position and took a look underneath the bed. He saw nothing under there though. He had high hopes that there was some form of entertainment in the room.

As he continued to check other areas in his assigned room, Bob stumbled across a chest. He thought it looked much like a treasure chest from a pirate story. With insatiable curiosity of what lies within he decided to open the chest.

As his curiosity grew to the point that he had to see the inside of the chest, he said his thoughts aloud, "I wonder what's in here," Bob asked himself. He hoped to find a chest full of gold." A get rich quick scheme entered his mind as quick as the speed of light once spotting the chest.

Bob turned out to be more than surprised when he saw what actually laid in the chest. He saw not one, but two ghosts in the chest, one on top of the other. Being transparent, it was more than easy to see them both.

Each ghost looked to be asleep and in the fetal position. Bob noticed that they were each female and looked to have a significant age difference. There was not any blood on either of them, and neither one moved.

Bob found himself in a state of shock. As he stared down at them, Bob failed to notice the

DRACULA

presence of a third ghost in the room. The third ghost was male and had a scar over his right eye. The ghost said in Romanian, "Stai acolo!"

Bob, not knowing Romanian did not realize that the ghost exclaimed, "Stay out of there!"

Bob new one thing, the male ghost looked angry. He put his hands out as if he was trying to use them as stop signs and slowly backed up.

Bob said to the ghost "I didn't mean to upset you." He continued as he said, "I don't want any trouble." As he was speaking, he picked up the pace slowly but steadily as he continued to back up. He reached down to grab his

DRACULA

luggage while backing up. It was unknown to Bob if any of his words were getting through. Bob quickly turned around and ran for the door. He moved faster than a runner running the dash, any yard dash amount. It almost seemed as if he was running on air it was hard to see his feet touch the floor.

DRACULA

Chapter 9

The Hallway Chat

All at once, Bob, Donna, Arnold, Janice, Frank, Mary and Alicia exited their rooms. Each of them was running in the direction away from their own bedroom doors. Each trying their best to escape the horrors they saw in their rooms.

Bob and Donna ran into each other in the middle of the hallway with their rooms being across from one another, each one exiting their rooms simultaneously. Janice and Arnold also ran into each other in the middle of the

DRACULA

hallway, their rooms too across from one another. This pattern was continued by Frank and Mary who too followed suit clashing into each other in the middle of the hallway.

All six of them, Bob, Donna, Arnold, Janice, Frank and Mary fell down as they bumped into one another in groups of two. Each one of them running into the one whose bedroom was on the opposite side of the hallway. The collision also knocked the luggage bag loose from Bob's hand.

As the six of them ran into one another they each said, "Uhf."

The odd ball of the bunch was Alicia. She did not have David to bump into in the middle of the hallway, being that he was not scared out of his room. Alicia therefore ran all the way from her room to David's bedroom door across from her own and quickly opened it.

Unintentionally she whipped the door open so quickly she bumped it into her face. The blow was light and for the most part shocked her as she stopped in her tracks. It still hurt though and she could not help but say, "Ouch."

Each of the six friends who ran into one another ended up each with simultaneous concern for their own health, as well as the health of each friend. Physical health was but the beginning from bumping into each other. The

DRACULA

physical health seemed to have been accompanied by psychological health.

Bob intended to run into Mary's arms, not Donna. Donna intended to run into Arnold's arms, not Bob. Arnold intended to run into Donnas' arms, not Janice. Janice intended to run into Frank's arms, not Arnold. Frank intended to run into Janice's arms, not Mary. Mary intended to run into Bob's arms, not Frank. Lastly, Alicia intended to run into David's arms, not David's door. None of them expected this. None of them knew what to expect next.

All the friends thought as someone scared would, running out the door and into the loving

DRACULA

arms of their betrothed. None of them though thought for a moment though that the one they were in love with was not directly across from them. That includes Alicia who too ran out her door, scared like the others.

Alicia found herself simply lucky in the situation to find that her man was assigned to the room directly across from her own. She however did not find herself in advantageous circumstances when her face met up with her beau's door as she swung it open.

The six friends who crashed unintentionally within the middle of the hallway, Bob, Donna, Arnold, Janice, Frank and Mary found that each of them now had mixed emotions come over them. These are emotions that none of them wished to have, nor neither admit to nor acknowledge. Even though it was neither admitted by anyone, nor acknowledged, a single question, a question of curiosity lingering in the back of their minds, "Who do I have stronger feelings for, is it the one I am betrothed to, or the one I ran in to?"

Not one of them was willing to speak the question. No one would so much as whisper the question. It simply remained as a thought in every individual mind, a thought that they tried to keep hidden in the back of their minds.

They did their best to keep it far from both their conscious as well as their subconscious. What we try to do is not always what we end up doing though.

With Bob, Donna, Arnold, Janice, Frank and Mary had new thoughts stir in their minds; and new emotions trying to but their way in on long pending emotions that stirred up. They each found new possibilities of emotional horizons opened up in only an instant to all six of them.

Not certain how to process all of their new thoughts and emotions, that began to run rapid. They all decided consciously and silently to try and do their best to suppress them until after their

DRACULA

trip. They all felt as though they were in a dangerous situation, and nobody wanted to create even more stress for the situation.

They got up rather quickly and noticed even faster that Alicia ran into an opening door. It was the door that leads to David's room. Mary, having the closest look asked, "Are you ok Alicia?"

As soon as they all stood up they walked Alicia's way. They were all in pain from their bumping into one another, but still they thought that Alicia got it worse. She did not run into a friend, but rather a hard wooden door; and wooden doors don't apologize for its actions. Rather, its actions are dictated by what we do with that door.

Alicia took a moment to respond as she was still in shock. As soon as the initial shock finally wore off she said, "I will be ok."

During all of this, David neither saw nor heard anything more than the opening of his door and the response of pain said by his fiancé. David decided as he heard the sound that a response was warranted. David said to the ghost whom he shared a room in Romanian, "Scuză-mă." David knew from his research that this Romanian message translated to "Excuse me." He then turned and headed to his door to see what was going on.

DRACULA

David promptly went to his door, with not any of his friends knowing whether or not he was in his room or not. With everyone else leaving from their rooms, it was a surprise that David, to their knowledge was unaccounted for. His friends shared a sigh of relief when they saw David at his bedroom door.

David saw Alicia at the door and hugged her. While hugging her he asked Alicia, "Are you okay sweetie?" He then continued by saying, "I heard a noise at the door." With curiosity looking in his mind he could not help but ask, "Why did you run into my door to begin with?"

Alicia was relieved to be in her beau's arms once again and found his concern a delight. She took comfort in his hallowed arms where she stayed to get a moments pleasure. Alicia did not answer David immediately as she took a moment to let the fear drain from her thoughts and tried replacing those thoughts with the joys of caressing arms.

A moment later, after feeling secure once again in his embrace Alicia answered, "David, I saw a ghost in my room. I ran for my life." She paused momentarily knowing that the ending of her statement was a bit embarrassing. Alicia then finished her explanation as she said, "And ran into your door, meaning to run into you."

Frank interrupted with a sigh of relief. Not intending to break up the sharing hugs moment. With Frank being the first of their six friends to get over to David's door he said to David, "Hey man, we thought you were a goner when we all ran out of our rooms and you were still in your room. We are glad to see you're okay."

David responded, "Thanks Frank. There is a ghost in my room. He is a deceased soldier from who knows when or where for that matter."

David was then interrupted by Frank again, this time it was while talking instead of hugging.

DRACULA

Frank asked with a surprised look on his face, "Do you mean to tell me that there is a ghost in your room too?" He paused for a second and asked, "And you didn't have the crap scared out of you like the rest of us?"

The other overheard the conversation as they made their way to David's room. Now, with everyone present and accounted for at David's bedroom doorway he answered, "Yeah, that's right Frank." David continued as he explained why he was not filled with fear at the sight of the ghost like his friends.

David told them, "The ghost in my room speaks Romanian. Since I studied Romanian, I was able to understand what the ghost was saying and I carried on a conversation with him."

David continued to explain, "You see, there are apparently ghosts here and there are two groups of them. There is a group that likes the idea of the curse so they won't end up in hell. Then there is the other group who wants the curse to end. They hope that once it ends they can go to heaven. It sounds like the two groups are pretty evenly split."

Janice then looked around and rhetorically asked, "I wonder if the ghosts are just limited to the bedrooms or if they could be in the other rooms too?"

Since nobody truly knew the answer nobody felt as though they could answer, rhetorical or not.

Arnold, after a moment of silence said, "I have a suggestion."

Mary, happy that her man had a suggestion on what to do decided to ask with a smile on her face, "What is it honey?"

Arnold responded, "Well, we simply explore the castle. We can check out the other two bedrooms, as well as the other four rooms more thoroughly."

Knowing that there were eight of them and still six possible rooms to check out, and a decision still needed to be made. They had three possibilities that Donna noticed immediately and decided

DRACULA

to share. She said, "I foresee three possibilities. Number one is that we can forget about looking for more danger and just stay put. Number two is that we do explore, but we all stay together in one big group. And of course number three is that we look around and split up, preferably into groups."

Looking around and splitting up was of course mentioned last because it was the last possible choice in Donnas' mind. David on the other hand thought that Donna saved the best idea for last.

David responded to Donnas' ideas by saying, "I think the last idea was the best." David went on to explain why he thought the last idea mentioned by Donna was the best of the bunch by saying, "If we split up we can cover more rooms at once and we can check out every secret about this hallway really quick. We should be able to be done with all the rooms separately and as quickly as it would take to check out one room all together."

Janice then decided to give her thoughts. She said, "You know, it seems to me that there are two more of us than there are rooms to still check out. Why don't we have one person to cover the four rooms on the end, and the other four of us split into teams of two to cover the last two bedrooms?" Janice's thought which was added to the mix

DRACULA

caught the intrigue of the rest of the group.

A new question occurred in Mary's mind. She decided to share her new question with the rest of the group as she asked, "How do we decide who check's out which room?"

Before anyone could directly answer Janice's question then, Donna had something she needed to mention. She said with a voice of concern and anxiousness, "All I know is that I got so scared I need to use the bathroom."

Arnold then said, "If we are going to volunteer for rooms, than I volunteer for the room next to the bathroom so I can keep an eye on Donna. I believe the room next

DRACULA

to the bathroom was the pantry and kitchen."

Frank decided to take a turn volunteering for room inspection next. He said, "I would like to check out what they have in the dining room. I am curious if their dining supplies are outdated or updated."

Frank's volunteering put Janice in a predicament. She did not want to be separated so she was next to volunteer for a room. She said, "If Frank is going to be checking out the dining room, than I want the common room." She then suggested, "Maybe Frank will join me when he is done with the dining room."

DRACULA

David noticed how the room selection was working out as did the others. David decided to keep the pattern going with couples taking rooms near each other. He said, "With the last two bedrooms left and four of us left I suggest that Alicia and I check out the bedroom next to mine. That leaves the other bedroom for Bob and Mary."

Bob was not saying much. He thought action would speak louder than words. Therefore his response was short and simple. He simply said, "Agreed."

Mary decided that it was her turn to either agree or disagree. Mary decided to comment, "I have no problem with that." Everyone was in agreement. The plans were set.

DRACULA

Chapter 10

Six Room Split Up

With the plans set, the friends separated and went to inspect their assigned rooms of the six remaining rooms not yet checked out. The two remaining bedrooms were the fastest to get to since they were on that end of the hallway. It took the others a moment to get to the other end of the hallway to inspect the remaining rooms down there.

Bob, Mary, David and Alicia waited outside their respective bedroom doors while the others made it to the other end of the hallway. They did their best to keep an eye on their friends for as long as they possibly could. With everyone at their doors they individually entered their rooms at the same time.

Arnold checked out the pantry. It seemed rather boring. He saw cupboards filled with shelves. On them were piles of canned goods with a can opener in the corner. Arnold felt it was a rather dull inspection. On other shelves he found boxed goods. As he spotted things in the pantry he named them off, speaking aloud in his lonesome.

Arnold first said, "Cans, cans and more cans." Then when he noticed the boxed goods he said to

DRACULA

himself, "Boxes, boxes everywhere. In seems there was not a shelf to spare." None of which he found though turned out to be refrigerated goods. He turned out to be glad of one thing and one thing only due to his inspection. Arnold was glad that he saw not a single ghost. Being finished with his room inspection Arnold headed toward the door.

Frank was across the hall from Arnold inspecting the dining room. It seemed unchanged from their earlier look. There was a huge dining table with candles to light it up. There was also a chandelier with lit candles to give the room a unique glow of flickering light and shadows of objects illuminating the room. One of the objects aglow from the candlelight was a china cabinet filled with china plates, bowls, saucers and silverware. To have the fanciest of tableware was no problem for royalty. The china looked aged, yet remarkably it was in fantastic condition. The only thought that Frank could put into words was, "Whoa!" Frank was glad that china was the only thing of interest he spotted. Seeing no ghosts he gladly headed toward the door to report his findings.

Meanwhile, on the other end of the hallway Bob and Mary inspect the bedroom on the end, next to Alicia's bedroom. Knowing ghosts like to hang out in the bedrooms they treaded cautiously. They did not notice immediately, but it didn't take much longer to notice what was just around the corner.

It was a male ghost soldier with not one, but two swords through him. He was pacing against the wall and seemed like he was trying to solve a problem that had an answer just out of the soldiers reach. The only thing that Bob and Mary noticed was the two swords in the ghost. One of which was through his heart. The other was through his ribs. Blood was all over his uniform from the piercing in his heart, as well as that of the ribs. The blood went all the way down to his boots.

DRACULA

The gore of the view made them both feel sick to their stomachs. The ghost neither said anything to them, nor even acknowledged that they were even in the room. Bob and Mary did their best to avoid doing something that would upset the ghost. The sight of the ghost stole both of their voices, but it lasted only for a moment. Bob and Mary began to tiptoe backwards, hoping to not make a single sound.

After taking a few steps they could not hold in their emotions any longer. The sight of blood filled both their eyes and their minds. Fear took over, fear that what happened to this soldier centuries outside of this time

DRACULA

would happen to them as well. Mary succumbs to her fears first. Unable to hold back what she had to say any longer, Mary screamed, "Aaaaaaahhhhhhh!"

Not a second after hearing her scream, Bob's fears ran to the surface and he shouted, "Ah!" Their fears were no longer kept in the solitude of their minds, but rather spoken with screams rather than words.

Just after the initial scream and shout they turned to run out the door. As they ran, Mary continued to scream, "Aaaahhhh!"

Bob could not hesitate to continue shouting either, "Aaahh!" It took very little time for them to reach their door.

DRACULA

Meanwhile, on the other side of the hallway, David and Alicia were inspecting the vacant bedroom next to David's room. They were spotted easily by a quick paced ghost in chains. The ghost was that of a male soldier stuck in the castle for hundreds of years. Agonizing daily over what was, and what could have been. His agonizing made him grow bitter and cold. His temper was matched only by the ferocity in his voice as he shouted, "Lasă aici acum sau blestemul asta al naibii de mine va cădea peste tine următor!"

David of course knew the translation and slowly backed away. Alicia followed suit and asked, "David, what did he say?"

DRACULA

David's heart pounded along with Alicia's. He whispered to her, "The ghost does not want us here. The ghost says," David then quoted the ghost, "Leave here now or the curse that damned me will fall upon you next."

As they continued to tiptoe backwards, Alicia asked another question that arose in her mind, "What do you think he means?"

David responded, "I'm not sure. And I don't think I want to find out." He paused for only a second and said, "All I can guess is that the entire castle is cursed and we may be its next victims. Either way, it's time to leave this room."

Alicia did not know what to make of what the soldier had to

say any more than David did. All she could think to do was to say, "I agree." The two of them turned together right away and ran for the door.

Back on the total opposite end of the hallway in the common room, Janice looked around. She saw book shelves with height surpassing hers. Books are on every shelf from end to end and wall to wall. Attached to the huge shelving unit is a ladder to help reach the higher up books. The ladder slides across the top from one end to the other. She felt as though she was in one of the largest libraries ever. She could not help but react by saying, "Whoa! That is a lot of books."

DRACULA

Books were not the only thing to be seen in this room. There was also relaxing furniture in the room. It was a selection of coffee tables, soft chairs and sofas. The floor was made of marble and glistened. The room's beauty was surpassing any expectations. Being a bookworm, Janice felt like she just entered a room where she could stay for quite a long time. It would take her years to read so many books. She grabbed one of the books off the shelf to see the condition of the books. It was an old book covered in dust and the title no longer legible. She blew at the book attempting to get off all the dust. Not able to see a title

DRACULA

she then opened the book and noticed it was not in English.

Shocked that there were so many books to choose from and not a single one legible she headed back toward the common room door with disappointment in her very heart. She said silently as she headed for the door, "I really wanted to read one of those books."

In the last of the unchecked rooms, Donna was checking out the bathroom. She had told her friends that she had to use the bathroom, which is why she got assigned the room to inspect. However, when she entered the room she did not even look for a toilet, or tissue paper. She noticed

DRACULA

nothing spectacular in the room. She did not even try to find anything in the room but one item. As soon as she saw it she said, "There is a mirror."

She raced over to the mirror and got out her compact. As she began to freshen up she noticed that her eyelash was not showing on her eyes in the mirror. She then asked herself, "What's wrong with this thing?"

Donna did not notice that the eyes staring back at her were not her own. Before she could take her eyes away from the mirror to inspect why her makeup was not working she found herself frozen in place. She was stuck, forced to keep staring at eyes that

DRACULA

were not hers. The eyes came closer and more body parts began to appear that were not Donnas'. Soon, an entire face appeared that Donna had never seen before. A voice came from the mouth as it began to move. Donna had no clue that she had run into the master of the castle. The voice said to Donna, "I, Dracula am your master now. You shall do as I bid. Your first mission shall be to eliminate the one who could suppress my spell on you."

DRACULA

Chapter 11

Donnas' Struggle

Donna knew who would best help her break the spell she now was trapped in. Unable to do anything else she headed for the door. Arnold was the one selected to be her first victim.

At the same time, Donna left her room calmly. Janice left her room upset. Arnold and Bob each left their rooms indifferent. David and Alicia, along with Bob and Mary each left their rooms with all four of them running out and smashing into each other in the middle of the hallway. David collided with Mary. Bob collided with Alicia.

Arnold, Frank and Janice heard the collision and raced to the other end of the hallway to see if their friends were alright. Donna headed that way too, not to check on her friends, but to follow Arnold. As they raced across the hallway Frank shouted, "Are you guy's okay?"

All four of them were tired of these head-on collisions. They had looks of being annoyed on their faces. The first to answer was Bob. He answered, "We should be fine. We just need to stop meeting like this. In my opinion, hallway collisions are really un-cool."

As they raced over, Donnas' pace was much slower. She seemed to move at the pace of a snail. There were no physical signs of anything being wrong, not even a limp. Looking back was Arnold in curiosity of what was taking Donna so long. Arnold asked loudly from one end of the hallway to the other, "What's taking you so long?"

Visions of Dracula laughed in Donnas' eyes. Meanwhile, Donna remained silent as she slowly continued walking. With every fiber of her being Donna tried to fight off Dracula's spell. She found herself to be not strong enough to break his control on her own. Dracula, deciding to use deceit talked to Donna through her mind from afar. He ordered Donna, "Reply to them. Make them think nothing has changed."

Doing as ordered by Dracula, Donna replied to Arnold, "I am fine. I am just tired from all the walking around we've been doing in this castle with no time to rest."

Arnold knew Donna to be much more energetic than the drab worn-out person he saw coming toward him from across the hallway. The other knew the same thing to be true, but only Arnold had a good look to see all of what was going on

Even Arnold, with the excellent view he had was still not good enough to notice the struggle

DRACULA

Donna had going on inside her. Not even Arnold could see that the reason Donna was moving so slow was because she was trying to stop Dracula from using her as a tool. She tried to remain still but Dracula was still able to make her move her legs, one step at a time.

Without realizing the struggle Donna had going on inside, Arnold was still able to see that something was wrong. Arnold did not believe that tired out story for one minute. Knowing Donna as well as Arnold does, he knew that she did not tire easily. Arnold decided to then ask her, "Are you sure it isn't anything else?" He continued as he said, "I know you, and it takes a lot more than walking around a

DRACULA

building, even if it is a castle for you to get tired out."

Dracula realized that Donnas' friends were not buying the lies that he was trying to sell. Dracula then gave new orders to Donna without anyone but Donna hearing. Dracula ordered, "Tell them, you are more than tired of looking through the castle. Tell them you are also bored. Searching rooms is not fun."

Donna then followed her new orders and said, "You're right. I'm not just tired out." She paused to try showing boredom then continued, "I am just getting bored looking around the castle. It's not as fun as doing things back home. Just looking through rooms, really,

DRACULA

can't we just find a quiet room and go to sleep?"

Dracula was sure that he had out-smarted her friends this time. While Dracula was trying to sell his lies, all four of Donnas' friends got back up from their collision and fall. Donna found herself being stared at by seven concerned faces. Arnold may have been the one with the best view, but they have all been friends for so long that more than Arnold found concern with what they saw and heard.

With Arnold leading the way, all seven of Donnas' friends decided to no longer wait for her to come to them as they began to walk to her. Arnold was the first one to get to where Donna was and threw his arms around her. Donnas' arms were trapped at her sides as Arnold gave her a big hug. While hugging Donna, Arnold whispered in her ear what she already knew, "I love you!"

Feelings overflowed Donnas' emotions. She was reminded of the love between Arnold and her, and she had yet to forget the hold Dracula has over her mind. Donnas' mind told her one thing, via Dracula, while her heart was telling her something else that was being reinforced by Arnold talking to and hugging her. Arnold could not keep Donna kept in the grasp of his arms as she used muscles of her own, enhanced by Dracula's grip to power out of the hug.

DRACULA

Donnas' eyes still had the image of Dracula within and she looked as though she had a crazed look upon her face. All seven friends were shocked about Donnas' new found muscles. No one was more shocked than Arnold since only he knew just how much strength he put into the hug. When Donna broke free of the hug she sent Arnold stumbling backwards a few steps but he did not fall. Arnold was so surprised he asked, "Whoa, how did you get so strong?"

Donna did not answer. She slowly crept closer to the stumbled Arnold. Donna raised her arms as she had devilish ideas run thru her mind thanks to Dracula. No one believed her raised arms were a sign of wanting a hug, especially after what she did during her last hug. Attempting to protect Arnold from what was controlling Donna, Frank said, "Don't worry, we got her."

Frank then ran behind Donna in an attempt to hold her from behind wrapping his arms around her waist. David helped as well by trying to hold back Donnas' left arm. Bob too got in on the action by trying to hold back Donnas' right arm. Janice then decided to attempt helping in her own way. She said to Donna, "I realize you may be angry about Arnold and me running into each other earlier. I'm sure you would much rather it was you he ran into. Remember, we were all running scared. We all just ran into whoever was closest. Arnold is still your man, and Frank is still my man even though he ran into Mary." She paused a moment than said, "Think," She continued by asking, "You don't want an accident that happened while panicking to come between you do you?"

Janice's words were reaching Donna. She realized that accident or no accident, she and Arnold are a couple. Dracula did not want to let her mind go though. He fought to keep her his mind slave. Dracula told her thru his mind control, "They lie! They all lie!

DRACULA

They are just afraid of what you will do to them. You must make Arnold pay for finding comfort in the arms of another woman! You must teach Arnold the scorn of a woman! It was his job to go to your arms, not hers!" Dracula felt he was clever. He reminded Donna of who Arnold ran into, and tried his best to suppress the memory of Donna running into anybody.

Arnold decided to take matters into his own hands. He felt the time for talk was at an end. Arnold believed that actions speak louder than words. Action therefore is what Arnold decided to try. He placed his left hand upon Donnas' right cheek. At the same time he placed his right hand upon Donnas' left cheek. Now, with holding her face still he went in for a kiss. It was no simple peck on the lips. It was a passionate kiss. Arnold could only hope that the kiss was passionate enough to overflow her emotions with love and drive out all the anger and spite Donna felt.

Arnold was unaware that Dracula was making her anger and spite increase tenfold. Arnold had faith he could bring Donna back no matter what made her so angry. Arnold kept his lips locked onto Donnas' until he felt she was kissing passionately back. During the passionate kiss, the intensity of strength Donna was putting out in order to free from the grip of Bob,

DRACULA

Frank and David lightened a little at a time. It continued until she was so enthralled with the kiss the she was like putty in Arnold's hands. As the intensity in Donnas' strength lessened, so did the grip Dracula had over her mind. Once she was putty in his arms being kissed, the control Dracula had over her had withered away to nothing.

David, Frank and Bob felt free to let go when they no longer felt Donna trying to break free. They stayed where they were just in case Donna was trying to use deceit to get out of their grip. When they let go, Donna could freely move her arms and wrapped

DRACULA

them around Arnold wanting the kiss to continue.

Bob said, "Okay, that's enough." Bob knew he was breaking up a kiss of passion but he had questions as did they all that they wanted answers to. Bob then asked, "Donna, why were you coming after Arnold like you were trying to kill him?"

Donna was confused. She had a puzzled look on her face and said, "I don't know what you're talking about." She continued as she tried her best to explain, "The last thing I remember was looking around the bathroom. After that I remember Arnold and I kissing until you broke up the kiss." With still a confused look she asked,

DRACULA

"But how did I get from the bathroom to Arnold's arms in the middle of the hallway?"

Everyone was surprised. How is it that Donna had no memory of attacking Arnold? Just as confused as the eight friends who are guests for one night in his castle, Dracula was equally confused. He asked his thoughts aloud, "How did she break my control? Is it truly possible that a mere kiss could break my powers of persuasion?"

DRACULA

Chapter 12

The Snack Attack

Since no questions got answered, all anyone could ask for was relief. Whatever was going on had ended and everything was back to normal, as it always should be. Frank, trying to release the tension began small talk by saying, "You know the dining room is pretty cool." He then suggested, "Maybe we could all go there to get a snack and unwind."

Frank's idea was liked by all. Donna replied, "If we are going to have snacks than we need to make a stop at the pantry too." She then asked, "Why don't you all go to the dining room and I'll get the snacks from the pantry?"

Donnas' suggestion was turned down immediately by Arnold. He replied in lightning quick fashion, "Oh, no. I'm not letting you out of my sight again quite so easily." Arnold paused then said, "I will go with you to the pantry. After all I was the one who checked out the room in the first place. While we gather snacks the others can check out the dining room."

Mary decided to get in on the conversation by saying, "Well, I guess that's settled."

With that they walked together back toward the pantry

DRACULA

and dining room. As they got close to the doors Arnold and Donna went toward the pantry while the others headed to the dining room.

As the friends separated to get a snack, the cunning wheels in Dracula's mind were turning quickly. The once prince was out for revenge. He wanted revenge for the betrayal he felt by Donnas' disobedience of his mind control. Dracula knew that Donna and Arnold would need to cross the hallway to get to the others in the dining room. With the friends occupying the two rooms Dracula set his plan of revenge in motion. While nobody was looking he set the bathroom door ajar. Dracula thought, the bait was set, now it was a matter of time until the fish took the bait.

David said, "This dining room looks much cooler when you actually take time to look at it."

Frank, being the original inspector of the dining room said, "Yeah, it looks cool when you first see it. After that though it gets a little boring seeing lots of candles and a table. You would think a prince could spring for more decoration."

As the conversation continued, Donna and Arnold left the pantry with handfuls of munchies. As they just started to cross the hallway they heard a door close. Neither was sure why

DRACULA

the door closed just then. All they knew was that the door they heard was the bathroom door. Arnold put out his hands and said, "Here, take these."

Arnold was referring to the snacks he was holding. Donna knew what he had in mind. She had a concerned look on her face. She knew that was the room where she lost her memory for a time. She took the snacks as asked and said, "Be careful."

Donna and Arnold then separated. Donna went to the dining room carrying the snacks. Arnold went to the bathroom to investigate why they heard the bathroom door close. Arnold knocked on the door and said,

"Hello!" He then asked, "Is anybody in here?"

He did not hear a response but just as certain someone was inside since he heard the door close and saw nobody exit. Arnold was puzzled as to why nobody responded. Finding himself in a puzzling situation enticed his curiosity. Arnold had two things he was curious of. He thought to himself, "Why is it that nobody answering? And who was inside?"

To satisfy his curiosity he slowly opened the door, hoping that whoever was inside the bathroom would not flash him. As Arnold slowly opened the door he asked again, hoping to get an answer this time, "Is anybody in here?"

Still, nobody answered. Arnold continued to enter the room slowly. He didn't notice anybody inside as he looked around. The room was empty accept for the few things a bathroom needs for use. Arnold thought it was nothing more than the wind blowing at the door which caused it to close. Feeling that there was no immediate danger Arnold put down his guard and lost his ambition to investigate the bathroom.

As he turned to head back out of the bathroom Dracula materialized behind him. Not realizing that he had company in

DRACULA

the room, Arnold was walking toward the door. Sneaking up from behind, Dracula saw his next meal in Arnold. Dracula lunged in with his fangs. The bite effected Arnold's central nerve system. It paralyzed his body while biting into the junction where Arnold's neck attached to his right shoulder. Dracula got his fill while Arnold was unable to move. It did not take long for Dracula to take enough blood from Arnold's body to have him bleed to death. With a corpse now in hand, Dracula decided to hide the body that was once Arnold.

Dracula dragged Arnold's corpse the rest of the way to the bathroom door. He then opened the door and continued to drag the body from the hallway where the friends were told to stay. After having pulled the corpse all the way through the door he used his ghostly talents to reclose the door. Dracula's right hand dematerialized and rematerialized on the door handle. Using his disconnected hand he closed the bathroom door. Dracula's hand then dematerialized from the bathroom door handle and rematerialized on his body.

Once that was taken care of, Dracula dragged the corpse that was once Arnold up the spiral stairway next to the hallway. The corpse was taken to the top of the stairway where there was another

DRACULA

door. He then opened the door at the top of the stairway and dragged the corpse inside. It was the tower. Inside was a pile if decayed bodies. Some were hundreds of years old. The newest to join the pile was that of Arnold which got thrown on the top of the bunch.

With the corpse no longer in hand, Dracula no longer needed to remain materialized for the task of holding things. With a grin he dematerialized. And with no body to use as a container any longer the blood Dracula collected from Arnold turned into a puddle where Dracula stood.

DRACULA

Chapter 13

Uncontrollable Emotions

Arnold's friends were beginning to get concerned. Arnold should have been back by now they thought. Donna was worried most of all. She suggested, "I think we should go see if Arnold is okay. After all, he has been gone a long time if all he was going to do is take a look in order to find out what caused the bathroom door to close."

Everyone else listened carefully as Donna made her

DRACULA

suggestion. They too knew that they should simply take a quick look and would have taken less time. Frank was first to reply to the suggestion Donna made by saying, "You're right. I think the bathroom needs looking into."

Donna replied, "My sentiments exactly."

Bob said, "Okay. We need to decide who will investigate the bathroom and who will stay here."

Donna said, "It's my beau who's missing. I will go to check it out." She then asked, "Will anyone come with me?"

Mary, understanding that it is hard to loose someone whom you care a great deal for and thought Donna could use a shoulder to cry on. She said, "I will go with you. Guys usually are not as sensitive as we girls are."

Donna replied "Thanks."

The others felt helpless as the two ladies headed toward the door. Mary and Donna were trying to give each other strength as they were holding hands while crossing the hallway. As they got to the bathroom door, Mary reached out to grab the handle. She took a deep breath and as she was getting ready to turn the knob she said, "Here we go."

Donna stepped inside first followed by Mary who was careful in leaving the door open. They stayed side-by-side and slowly walked through the room. Donna

DRACULA

called out, "Arnold! Are you here honey?!"

There was no answer. They knew by the time they were halfway into the room they should have been able to see Arnold. Not hearing him respond just affirmed their thoughts. Mary said after a moment of silence, "I don't think he's in here. I can't see Arnold, and he didn't respond either."

Worry was in both ladies eyes and hearts. Neither could understand why it was so hard to find the whereabouts of Arnold. Together they slowly backed up and out of the room. As they backed out of the bathroom and found themselves back in the hallway facing the door to the

DRACULA

bathroom they closed the door in front of them very quickly. Mary and Donna then turned and ran across the hallway and back to the dining room.

When the two ladies arrived back in the dining room, relieved to see that no one else went missing in their absence they found themselves each out of breath. Unknown to the others of why the ladies were out of breath but glad to see that they were unharmed Bob asked them, "Well, what happened?"

After taking a moment to catch their breath, Mary was the first to answer, "We were unable to find Arnold. That's what happened."

DRACULA

With a worried look upon his brow David looked down, trying to hide his looks of worry his eyes told ever so well. Much to his own surprise David found himself looking down and trying to be helpful in another way. He saw on the ladies shoes something red. He asked, "Mary, Donna, what did you two step in?" He continued as he explained the reason for his question, "I was just wondering because there is something red on your shoes."

Neither Mary nor Donna noticed anything on the floor to step in while in either room. They were each surprised to hear their shoes were even dirty. They looked down at practically the same time to see what David was talking about. Not realizing it at the time they had stepped in blood.

When they spotted the blood on their shoes they were both grossed out. Mary had a weaker stomach when it came to the sight of blood compared to Donna. Donna however knew the blood had to come from somewhere. The last person whom she knew to be in the room before Mary and herself was Arnold.

Donnas' eyes began to water. The reality of what happened to Arnold began to surface. She came to the realization that the kiss she got to break Dracula's mind control would be the last kiss she would receive from her beau.

DRACULA

Donna did not wish to show her feelings so quickly, but she could not help but think she had to be strong to honor Arnold's memory. With feelings of pain due to the reality of her loss and her feelings of trying to honor his memory racing through her, at the same time she then lost control of her emotions. Donna went from being watery eyed to falling down to her knees with her arm over her eyes crying profusely.

Bob wanted to help. He knelt down in front of Donna and wrapped his arms around her. Bob looked at it as nothing more than trying to comfort a friend. Donna looked at it as a friendly shoulder to cry on. Mary had a

DRACULA

different outlook on the situation. She felt betrayed. She asked herself in her mind only, "Why is he comforting her instead of me? I was with her in the bathroom and got blood on my shoes too. Doesn't he care about me anymore?"

With her thoughts of anger and rage building up, Mary stormed out of the room. She told nobody where she was going or why she was leaving the room. Thoughts of betrayal put fire in her eyes. It was a fire like she had never felt before. Everyone heard the door slam as Mary exited the room.

Alicia ran to the door to see what was going on. She was too late to see where Mary had gone.

DRACULA

Mary was no longer in the hallway, and not knowing which room Mary entered, Alicia could follow her no further.

As Alicia stepped back into the room and David asked, "So where did Mary go?"

Alicia, with a look of concern on her face said, "I'm not sure. When I looked in the hallway she wasn't there." She paused a moment then continued, "My guess is she went into another nearby room."

As the discussion in the dining room continued, Mary was in the next room over, the common room. Mary paced in the common room at quite a fast pace. She had mountains of anger to burn off and she felt, the sooner the better. Her pacing was in an oval shape next to some furniture.

Unknown to Mary, she was being watched with intrigue by Dracula. He was undecided whether or not to attack her. Dracula thought if he left her alone her rage would get the better of her making her lash out at the others. There was a part of him that thought she may not take her rage out on the others and she changed rooms in order to cool off. This was the reason he looked with intrigue and was undecided. Mary's anger made it hard for Dracula to read her mind. It was unknown to Dracula whether or not he could use her as an instrument of destruction.

Before Dracula could decide what to do, with the same angry face still upon Mary's brow she left the common room and entered the hallway. She slammed the door behind herself in the wake of her exit. Mary continued walking through the hallway back to the door of the dining room. Mary put out her hand as she grabbed the door knob. She then took a deep breath and exhaled. After taking the deep breath she let most of her anger leave with the exhaled breath.

Chapter 14

Missing Mary

The discussion Mary missed out on was still in progress. Frank asked no one else in particular, "I wonder how Mary is after she stormed off?"

Before anyone could answer there was a scream coming from the hallway. What nobody knew was that Dracula had materialized behind Mary. Everyone had hunches as to who screamed, but knowing that something happened to Arnold already they were not certain if their hunches were correct. The scream sounded like

DRACULA

Mary, this much they were certain of. What nobody was certain of was who or what killed Arnold. The killer could have been female as easily as it could have been male. They knew the bedrooms for certain were filled with ghosts and that there was something in the bathroom.

What nobody knew happened on the other side of the door was Dracula grabbing both of Mary's arms from behind. Mary was frozen in fear accept to scream from the top of her lungs. With Mary frozen in fear and putting up not a single fight, that Dracula was free to go in for the kill. Dracula did the same thing to Mary as he did to Arnold. Using his fangs he bit into the junction connecting her neck and right shoulder. He slowly drained the blood. Dracula found that estrogen filled blood was tastier than testosterone filled blood. To him, it tasted more like gourmet.

Dracula drained enough to make Mary pass out but not die. While her neck was being punctured and sucked dry her scream was being silenced, as it was when she passed out. Being passed out Dracula was able to take her with ease from the hallway and up the spiral stairway. Once at the top she too was taken to the tower room where there was a bed of decaying corpses. He laid her on the floor next to the pile of corpses that made a bed for Arnold's corpse to decay with.

Meanwhile, when the scream was heard through the door of the dining room, not only wasn't anybody certain it was Mary screaming, they were also not certain the reason for the scream, because the scream seemed to stop early. It only lasted but a couple of seconds. They know a female scream when they are in danger and they scream for as long as they can, as loud as they can. This common sense information told them that something was wrong.

Alicia asked, "What was that?"

David wanted so much to comfort Alicia. In hopes of doing

so he said to her, "I'm not sure." He paused then decided to give guesses, "It could be either Mary crying for help. Or it's possible that it wasn't Mary at all. It could have also been whoever killed Arnold is trying to lure us out of the dining room."

Bob decided to butt in and give his own thoughts. Interrupting David, he said with guilt in his voice, "Or it could still have been Mary. She may be mad at me for comforting Donna instead of her when they came back from their bathroom inspection."

There was silence for a moment as everyone pondered each possibility. Donna, feeling guilty that she got the attention from Bob instead of Mary getting Bob's attention began to cry. Tears ran down her face and she began to sniffle. The others were not certain if her actions were due to the loss of Arnold, or the absence of Mary.

Noticing a tear run down Donnas' cheek, Bob put his index finger on her cheek to catch the tear. He then asked, "Why are you crying?"

Donna replied, "I feel like I'm the reason that Mary left like she did. Now I'm not sure if she's alright. If anything happens to her I feel as though I'm responsible."

The others understood what Donna meant. They all felt like

cowards for not looking in the hallway in order to discover for certain the cause of the scream. Not one member of their group knew if Mary was still alive or just as dead as Arnold. That was eating away at all their consciences. All that each of them could do was hope; hope that Mary was somehow alright wherever she was.

Although all understood, it was Bob who started the conversation, and it was Bob who carried the conversation on. He replied, "I see." He paused for just a moment as he gave Donna a hug then said, "You are not the only one who feels that way." He paused for a moment more and said, "We all feel guilty for letting her storm off. No matter which one of us took point, one of us should have stopped her."

Bob's message calmed Donna, but did not relieve her of the guilt she felt. Donna had tears coming down her face, thinking only the worst possible scenario. She was ready to reply to what Bob said. Before she got the chance to do so, Janice interrupted their private conversation that was not as private as they were surrounded by their friends. Janice said as she abruptly interrupted, "No matter what you think Donna and you too Bob, none of us could have stopped Mary from taking off." She paused then continued as she explained,

"None of us knew she was planning on running out of the room like that."

Before Janice could say anything else to calm her friends she too found herself interrupted. The one interrupting Janice was David who said, "Janice is right. We've all been friends for so long. None of us would have guessed that she would have a meltdown like this."

Feeling panicked from uncertainty Bob replied, "We need to find her! I need to know if she is dead or alive!"

Alicia, feeling it was her turn to try to comfort a friend said, "We will do what we can. I didn't see her in the hallway when I

DRACULA

looked. She didn't have time to go far. That tells me she has to be in one of the other rooms closest to here."

With hope in their hearts and doubt in their minds they decided to rely on their hope. The first to respond to Alicia was Bob who replied, "Well, that's a start at least."

David, thinking of which rooms are closest and would be considered safest helped him think of a way to narrow down their search perimeter. He shared his thoughts aloud with the others as he said, "Okay, we know there are ghosts in each of the ten bedrooms. We also know the bathroom was the last room Arnold was in before

DRACULA

he was killed." He paused for a moment as everyone was given a chance to remember their lost friend. He then continued, "We are in the dining room. That leaves only the pantry and the common room as places here I might go to."

Everyone started to feel better with their search narrowed from thirteen possible rooms to check all the way down to two. Feeling better with a clearer picture of possible places to check Frank had an idea. He said, "There are six of us, and two rooms to inspect. It seems like pretty easy math to me. We split up into teams of three." He paused a second as he thought of whom to team with whom.

Not waiting to hear his idea of teams Bob said his own, "I think it would be a good idea if Donna and I were a team since it is our sweethearts who are missing, if not dead. But, if we are going to have teams of three though we need a volunteer to come with us and whoever is left is the other team of three."

The idea was liked by all. Janice said, "I'll go with you two. You both might want shoulders to cry on."

David then said to Frank, "Well that leaves me, you and Alicia."

DRACULA

Janice then said, "I was the one to inspect the common room earlier. Since I am familiar with it I think my team should take it."

Donna and Bob had no objection. David replied, "That's fine with me. It would give me and my team a chance to check out the pantry for ourselves."

Unrealized by all of her friends, Mary was not in either room. As Dracula was planning his next victim, he nearly forgot that Mary was not dead yet. The smell of fresh blood lingered in the air of the tower. Mary was beginning to feel better. She went from unconscious to stirring, attempting to wake up. Mary still felt weak and cold from the loss of blood.

DRACULA

How Mary felt though was of no concern to Dracula. He saw her as nothing more than the next meal, a meal he wanted to take his time eating.

Dracula was disappointed that Mary began to stir. He knew that if she screamed loud enough, the location of his victims could be revealed to this group of outsiders. Dracula knew what needed to be done in order to keep secret his hidden location of victims. He picked Mary back up with ease. Still weak and unable to fight back Mary found herself in Dracula's mercy. Dracula had no mercy though. He was royalty that feasted on the blood of his fallen enemies. To him, what was one more body? He stuck his fangs in her yet again, this time draining the last of her blood from her already weakened body.

Once he was done with her, she was tossed like a rag doll onto the pile of decayed bodies. She did not land on top of Arnold directly but beside him. With no longer a concern to keep a lid on her voice Dracula felt it was time to now spy on her friends. He wanted a closer look at each one of them. Dracula wanted to decide whom to prey on next. Dracula then dematerialized, leaving behind a puddle of blood.

DRACULA

Chapter 15

The Search for Mary

One at a time the group of friends left the dining room. Frank said to Bob and team, "Good luck."

Janice, feeling the wish of luck was directed to her only responded, "Good luck to you too."

Each of the groups headed toward the doors of the rooms where they were going to look for Mary in. Acting like a gentlemen, David grasped the handle of the pantry. He then opened the door and said, "After you."

DRACULA

Alicia was flattered at the gesture and the first to enter the room. She was followed by Frank. While Alicia was entering the room, passing her boyfriend David, she had a look in her eyes and said, "Thank you."

The look was one of those looks that was worth a thousand words. Alicia was not only impressed how David could act like a gentleman with all that has happened. Alicia was also impressed that he was keeping his cool, knowing one friend was dead and possibly a second friend as well.

As Alicia was going by, David took notice watching as he stared at her butt he said, "Don't mention it."

Frank's entrance blocked David's view. Frank realized what David was up to as well. It was not his wish to deprive David of his view but he knew they both needed to enter and the search must take place. Being polite as he entered Frank too said, "Thank you."

David knew with Alicia going first his view would get blocked by Frank. It didn't matter to David though as long as he had the opportunity to stare, if only for a moment. David too continued being polite as he said, "It's quite alright." Then David entered and closed the door on his way in.

DRACULA

Bob noticed from across the hall the suave moves that David was attempting to use on Alicia and decided to try some moves out also. With a grin on his face Bob took the handle to the common room door and opened it for the ladies as a gentleman should. He then said, "After you ladies."

Both ladies felt flattered by the gesture, Donna more than Janice. Although Janice would have preferred the gentleman's actions be done by her own man she still felt as though thanks were in order. Janice entered first and as she passed, she said, "Thank you."

Donna entered next and as she got to the door she decided to take thanks to the next level. Donna decided that even though she was not in a dress, she would still act like a lady in return of Bob's being a gentleman. She did a curtsy and said, "Why thank you sir."

Donna then entered the room without realizing that the gentleman was Bob, who had already ended as he stared at her backside as she entered the room. Bob followed as he stared at her butt and closed the door after entering the room himself. While staring, Bob replied, "My pleasure." Neither of the ladies realized how much pleasure Bob was referring to.

DRACULA

The common room looked a little dim. There were torches all over the room in order to keep it well lit, but it seemed some of them went out. Concern of attacks in the dark entered each of their minds. Not one of them knew why the room was dim. Thoughts changed in a hurry from flirty to worry. Bob put out each hand, one for each of the ladies to grab. He then said, "Let's stay together."

Janice reached out and grabbed his left hand, while Donna reached out and grabbed his right hand. Together, they walked slowly to an unlit torch. Janice, being the closest reached out and grabbed the torch. With the torch

DRACULA

in hand they pressed onward to another torch, a lit torch. Janice said, "We need to stop for a minute so we can relight this torch."

Silently Bob and Donna agreed with a nod. Janice put her arm out to relight the torch and was successful. After relighting the torch Janice said, "Okay, it's lit."

Still holding hands they began to walk backwards. They backtracked all the way to the place where the torch was taken from its wall mounting spot. With everyone realizing where they were, Bob let go of both ladies hands and reached for the torch. As he reached for the torch he said, "I'll remount the torch."

DRACULA

Janice handed the torch over to Bob. Watching with concern in her eyes Donna said, "Be careful."

Bob was flattered that Donna was showing so much concern for his wellbeing. With a grin on his face and his back facing the ladies he mounted the torch back up.

Unknown to Bob, it was his turn to be the one getting watched. Donna and Janice watched with interest wondering if Bob could remount the torch without getting burned. Donna had a second reason to stare all her own. Her second reason was the main reason she watched and stared. Donna wanted to see the tightening of muscles as Bob stretched out his arm revealing the muscles in both his arms and his back.

As Bob set the torch back into its spot on the wall, Donna said, "Nice muscles." Embarrassed that she was revealing her true interest she tried to quickly take back what she said. Trying to correct what she had just said a split second later she said, "I mean nice job."

Even though Donna tried her hardest to cover up what she had said to Bob, neither his hearing nor Janice's was bad. Try as she might to cover up her intended thoughts, Donna failed miserably. Now knowing her thoughts as directed towards his muscles, Bob grinned. As he turned around he said, "Thanks." After a slight momentary pause he said, "You've got some nice muscles yourself."

Janice decided that a new topic was in order before Donna and Bob started comparing other body parts. Her mind raced to stay out of the gutter as she chose a new topic for discussion. Remembering where they were and why Janice said, "Now, let's see if we can find Mary, or at least a clue as to where she went."

With the reminder of why they were where they were, Donna and Bob had to find within themselves restraint. Donna was the first who responded to Janice's reminder by saying, "You're right.

DRACULA

With the room relit we can see better now. Let's get to work."

Bob of course had felt that he too should assure Janice that his mind was on the topic at hand. To assure her he said, "Let's find out what we can."

Assured that they were back to the topic on hand, Janice was relieved. Janice had relief for not just one reason, but two. The first was that Janice was relieved she would no longer have to hear the sexual taunts going on in the room. The second thing she found relief in was that she would not need to search the room along while sexual advancements were attempted in the same room. Being relieved, Janice said, "Thank you."

Together they slowly moved throughout the room. With the room well lit it was obvious that there was no sign of Mary. They each knew though that if Mary had been in the room earlier that it is possible that she left behind a clue as to where she may have gone. With six eyes peeled for the slightest clue nobody dared to even blink.

They checked for a note. They checked for splattered blood. They even looked for Mary's clothes wondering if she got hurt, were her clothes torn too. They were unable to find a trace of her in the room. This gave them mixed emotions. Nobody was sure if they should be happy that no evidence was found, or worried that they were unable to find her, or a clue to her location.

As their search was finalized, Bob said to both Donna and Janice, "It looks like there are no clues here. I hope David, Alicia and Frank had better luck."

Meanwhile, across the hallway in the pantry David said as he entered, "So this is where they found the snacks. Well, let's see if there is more to this room than just some snacks."

Walking slowly and cautiously Alicia read David's mind. Believing she knew what he would say next she added, "And see if we can find a trace of Mary."

Frank found it cute how Alicia was finishing David's thoughts. Frank found it so cute he cracked a smile and let out a small and quiet laugh. After his little laugh, Frank said, "You two should go do a comedy act some time. All you would need is a really big outfit and pretend you are Siamese twins. One head could start talking, and the other head finishes the sentence." He then asked, "What do you think, cool huh?"

David found it surprising that Frank would even make such a suggestion as did Alicia. David responded to Frank's idea by saying, "Just because we finish each other's sentences from time

DRACULA

to time doesn't mean we are putting on an act."

Alicia then responded with words of her own, "And besides, we don't wear clothes the same size as a human aquarium."

Frank laughed again, harder and longer this time. While Frank was laughing, he tried his best to say his thoughts, "There you go again." He continued as he asked, "Do you always start David and let Alicia finish? Or do you switch roles sometimes?"

Neither David nor Alicia found any humor in Frank's jokes. Doing her best to not let Frank's wise cracks affect her, Alicia said, "That's enough. We came here to look around for Mary, not make bad jokes."

Frank stopped laughing immediately. His quitting laughing though was not due to the request of Alicia. Frank's laughter stopped because he found no humor in being told that his jokes were bad. Hurt feelings extinguished Frank laughter, and now everyone in the room felt the same. Each of them was a recipient of a joke or insult and did not like it one bit. Time for laughter was at an end.

Reminded that the reason they were in the room was to find Mary and not make jokes put everyone back in the mindset they needed to conduct a thorough search. They looked around,

DRACULA

above, and even beneath boxes. There was neither a drop of blood, nor a torn piece of clothing to be found. Everyone felt discouraged. They had hoped that at least a clue would be found if not Mary herself.

Frank, in disappointment said, "No Mary. Not even a clue to where Mary is."

Alicia said, "Let's hope the others had better luck than we did."

David then said, "They had to. There is no way that there was no clue in either room."

Frank noticed quite quickly what had just happened. He then said to David, "I guess you do finish her sentences sometimes too."

No longer wanting to talk about who finishes who's sentences David said, "Come on. Let's go see if the others made better progress than we did."

David headed toward the door followed by Alicia with Frank coming up the rear. As David and company headed toward the pantry door, unknown to them Bob and company was headed to the common room door at the same time. David opened the pantry door. As he held open the door he said, "After you." As he spoke he made an arm gesture indicating exactly where to go.

DRACULA

Frank walked through first. As he did he whispered, "This time I won't block your view."

After Frank left the room Alicia began to exit the door. She said to David before exiting, "What a gentleman."

The compliment put a smile on David's face. He replied sarcastically, "Why, thank you very much."

Alicia then left the pantry with a sexy taunt walk. David liked what he saw as he stared at her during her exit. As soon as the doorway was clear he followed behind Alicia with his eyes remained fixated on her posterior. David then closed the door after he too left the pantry.

DRACULA

Meanwhile, Bob being the only man in the group across the hall in the common room knew he was the only one in his group to be a gentleman. Doing his best to be one under the current circumstances Bob grabbed the door handle. He opened the door and said, "Ladies first."

Janice said, "Thank you." She then walked through the doorway, back to the hallway.

Donna was next to go through the doorway. With mixed emotions she stopped walking as she got next to Bob. Donna did not want to disrespect Arnold's memory, at the same time she still had a life to live. She hoped it would be long and fruitful. With her mixed emotions she needed to decide how to act. Donna knew that she had lost Arnold, and that Bob had lost Mary. It only seems natural that they try to hook up.

Acting on her emotions after a moment Donna wrapped her arms around Bob's neck and went in for a kiss. Bob was more than accepting of the kiss and kissed back. The kiss lasted only a few seconds, but with emotions running all over in both of their minds the few seconds felt like time standing still. When they unlocked the lip-lock Donna said, "You were very brave. Never lose that."

Bob was slightly surprised about both the kiss and the

comment. Even though the kiss came as a surprise he had no regrets in taking part of the kiss. Bob was also surprised about Donnas' comment. He wondered what he did to warrant comments of admiration. Instead of asking though, Bob went with the flow and replied, "Why, thank you."

Donna then walked through the door, peaking behind herself to stare at Bob as he left the room next. Bob closed the door on his way out. Bob too had a stare of his own. Bob's stare was forward though, as opposed to Donnas' backwards stare. With Bob exited from the common room, everyone who was left was in the hallway.

DRACULA

Chapter 16

Bob's Investigation

With both groups in the hallway it was time to compare notes. David, Alicia and Frank started to walk across the hallway toward the dining room. Bob, Donna and Janice noticed which door the others were heading toward and began to head to the same door.

Then, all of a sudden, Janice decided to break away from her group with Bob and Donna. Instead of heading toward the dining room door, she ran as fast as possible with her arms wide

DRACULA

open directly toward Frank wanting a hug. Frank was a bit surprised that Janice couldn't wait for a hug until they met up at the door, but it was a surprise that he was more than happy with. As soon as her arms were wrapped around Frank and his arms wrapped around her in return Janice said, "I missed you."

Frank loved the fact that he was getting overwhelming attention from just a few minutes of separation. Frank felt all he could do was reply, "I missed you, too."

In attempting to calm Janice down, Frank went one step further than just a hug. After his reply Frank kissed Janice on the forehead. Frank could only hope that his plan to calm Janice down would work. What Frank did not know was how Janice would react to his response and forehead kiss. A good reaction of calming down is all he could hope for.

Janice's heart rate was beginning to return to normal. She looked deep into Frank's eyes and said, "Thank you." Before giving Frank a chance to reply Janice wanted to return the kiss. She however had no intention of a kiss on the forehead. Due to Frank being taller, Janice got up on her tiptoes and planted one right on the bull's-eye that is Frank's lips.

Once Frank's lips were no longer being held hostage by

DRACULA

Janice's lips Frank felt free to respond, "You're welcome." He paused but a moment and said, "Thank you for a great kiss."

Once the hugging and kissing was over, they were able to continue their way to the dining room. The first to the door was Bob. He opened the door and made a hand gesture with his hand as an open palm showing everyone where to go. He then said, "After you."

One-by-one the others walked through the opened door. Donna being right beside him was first to enter. Next to arrive at the door was David and Alicia. David said to Alicia, "After you."

Alicia was flattered by the gentleman qualities David possessed. Alicia wanted to return such politeness with a lady-like response. She replied, "Why thank you sir."

Alicia then entered followed by her beau, David. Next to arrive at the door were Frank and Janice. Janice predicted that Frank would follow suit and be a gentleman letting her go first. Janice had other plans though. She got to the door slightly before Frank and said, "Age before beauty."

Frank found Janice's remark to be cunning. He knew, just as well as she did that he was only months older than she was. Not to cause an argument; and to admire her cunning attempt to get him to enter the room first, all he could do was say, "Thank you. I wouldn't want the doorway to corrupt your beauty before it could guess my age." With a smile on his face, Frank then entered the dining room followed by Janice, his beauty.

With everyone else entered, Bob was next to be entering the room and close the door after he entered. Bob did close the door, but he did not enter the dining room first. All of the sudden, Bob ran to the end of the hallway where they first entered the hallway. He knew bodies didn't just disappear. Bob was determined to find out just where the bodies of his Mary went as well as the body of his friend Arnold. The only thing he was certain of was that they had to be somewhere in the castle. They were not in the places already checked which narrowed down the possibilities in his head.

When he got to the end of the hallway Bob was panting from trying to sprint there. As he tried to catch his breath he looked around. He noticed the spiral stairway and a light bulb lit up in his mind. He figured the others must have either gone up there to explore or that there was someone else in the castle who took them up there somehow. Saying his thoughts aloud Bob said, "They have to be up there."

As Bob slowly began up the stairway the others ran to the dining room door. The first to the door was Donna. She grabbed the handle and flew the door open. Donna then ran out to the hallway followed by the rest of the group. Knowing nobody had the answer to her question Donna rhetorically asked, "Where did Bob go?"

Janice, not taking the question to the rhetorical face value that was intended answered, "Not a clue. I don't see him anywhere."

All of a sudden Donna felt alone once again. She then said,

DRACULA

"Oh no. My guess is that Bob was taken just like Arnold then Mary."

As the friends kept looking around, Bob was still panting as he walked up the stairway. They were looking for any door that may be ajar. Bob made it all the way to the top of the stairway and gazed upon a door. Unknown to Bob, not only did he find the right place, but he was in more danger now than ever before.

Dracula materialized right behind Bob. Keeping his ghostly body levitated he bit into Bob's neck and shoulder connection on the right hand side just as Bob reached for the handle. Bob found his body stuck in total paralysis as his blood was drained ounce by ounce. Once every ounce was sucked dry from Bob's veins, Dracula stopped sucking and threw Bob's dried out carcass over his shoulder. Dracula then opened the door to his tower room. He carried the carcass of Bob's empty shell of a body to his pile of decaying carcasses. Dracula then dropped the raggedy body that once was Bob on the top of his pile.

Dracula's pile of empty, soulless bodies had gotten so high now and so uneven that Bob's empty shell rolled off the top of the pile like dead weight tumbling down the stairs. As Bob's empty shell went tumbling down, the right arm of his empty shell swung with falling momentum and hit Dracula in the back of the head.

The hit in the head barely had any effect on Dracula accept to anger him. With his anger raised he decided to take out his vengeance. First, Dracula said, "How dare you!" Dracula knew he was talking to a dead body, but he didn't care. Dracula had rage from getting hit and wanted to take it out on the one who hit him.

Dracula then picked up the fallen corpse that was once Bob's body and bit into him yet again. This time he made sure to suck out the very last drop of blood. Dracula then threw the now empty corpse to the floor. Dracula then turned his eyes crimson red and laughed devilishly happy for getting his vengeance on the empty corpse. Dracula continued laughing as he became transparent once again, letting the blood splash to the floor. Dracula's laugh echoed through the tower, "Wa, ha, ha!!!!"

DRACULA

Chapter 17

The Room Transfer

As Dracula's sick and evil laugh continued unheard by the group of friends in the dining room, many were feeling uneasy. Alicia was the first to speak out about feeling uneasy as she said, "I'm scared." She then paused as her heart jumped a beat. A small amount of tears began to run down her face. As the tears began, Alicia continued by saying, "I don't think we are safe in this room anymore."

David, being her boyfriend put the largest amount of

concentration and concern in the frightened voice of Alicia. David responded, first physically followed by verbally. David put his hands on Alicia's arms, and stared her straight into her teary eyes. David then said to Alicia, "I understand that you are frightened. If it will make you feel better we could all head to my assigned bedroom."

David was hoping for a response from Alicia. He kept holding her and staring in her eyes. A response was given, but not by the one he expected it to come from. The response was said instead by Frank. He responded, "I do recall you being the only one who didn't run scared from their bedroom. That just might be a good idea."

When David heard a response coming from Frank he let go of Alicia and paid attention to Frank and his response.

Janice then said, "I agree. We need to get to a place where nobody has disappeared from."

As everyone seemed to be in agreement Alicia said, "All right, that seems to be settled. Let's get out of here and head down to David's room."

David was the first one to get to the door and held it open like a gentleman. Once the door was open he said, "After you."

Donna, the one who felt like a black widow spider was first to *go through the door held open by David. Not knowing who would die next, or if anyone would survive the night, the cheerful attitude of young love and overzealous adventure has been tamed. Donna simply said "Thank you." She then walked through the door and waited silently in the hallway as she knew she would be followed out by the others one-by-one.*

Janice was next in a small line of friends to exit the room with David holding the door. Janice, not feeling like a black widow spider, yet sad to see her friends missing tried her best not to allow her feelings to be known as she smiled and said, "Thank you David."

Janice was followed out by her beau, Frank. Frank was much less emotional than the two ladies who left the dining room already. Frank's idea was to say as he was getting ready to head out the door, "Don't worry, we will get through this."

David was still holding the door open for his girlfriend, Alicia. Alicia did not want to separate from David for any reason. Seeing to it that separation was not an option Alicia grabbed David's free hand and said, "Come on. Let's walk out of here together."

A smile was cracked by David as he replied, "Okay." Side-by-side while holding hands, David and Alicia walked through the door. David then closed the door behind himself as he and Alicia left the dining room. Once everyone was in the hallway David said, "Now, let's head down to my assigned room." Everyone began to walk slowly down the hallway then David thought that he forgot to mention something. What he forgot to mention just came back to him after moving only a few steps. He then finished what he needed to say a few moments ago by saying, "And keep your eyes peeled for anything out of the ordinary."

DRACULA

Frank, wanting to act all macho replied, "Duh, that's a little obvious."

Janice found her beau's sarcastic remark funny and did her best to keep her laugh silent, "He, he, he, he, he!"

Unknown to any of our friends; they were all being both watched and heard. The spying began at the opening of the dining room's door. Being able to materialize and dematerialize, Dracula came up with a horrifically ingenious spying idea.

After dematerializing in the tower, he decided to materialize only his eyes and ears. This time though was unlike any other time yet. Dracula materialized his left

DRACULA

ear and left eye at the end of the hallway on the left side. He also materialized his right ear and his right eye at the end of the hallway on the right side. Doing so, he was able to see where they were going and hear their plans.

Although the friends kept their eyes peeled, they were looking for the cause of their friend's disappearances, not very small body parts that are hard to see from a distance. The small body parts are behind them as well, making them that much harder to notice.

As soon as they arrived at David's assigned bedroom door, David opened it and said, "Come

DRACULA

on in and close the door after everyone's in."

David was followed by Alicia. Next to enter was Janice, followed by Frank. Last but not least to enter was Donna. As she was last to enter she closed the door on her way in. The soldier ghost that David was conversing with earlier was still there. When the ghost saw Donna, he was in awe. David noticed the shock, expressed from the soldier ghost. David asked him in Romanian, "Ceea ce este gresit?"

Alicia then asked David before the soldier had a chance to respond, "What did you say?"

David explained, "I just asked the soldier here, what is wrong?"

DRACULA

The soldier hoped their little private conversation was over. He decided either way, it was time that he spoke up and answered the question. He answered by saying, "Cel care a intrat în ultima, arata ca o în pictură."

Alicia then said, "Translation please."

David answered, "He said the one who walked in last, looks like the one in the painting." David then asked the ghost in Romanian, "Ce vrei să spui? Ce pictura?" David then took the time to explain, "I just asked, "What do you mean? What painting?"

The soldier replied, "Este o pictura de pe Printul Vlad Dracul nevasta. El a pierdut la tragedie şi a fost căutarea pentru sufletul ei să fie renaşte într-un corp nou atunci. Persoana care a intrat în camera de ultima, se pare ca cel din pictura."

David was shocked. He knew his friend who entered his assigned room last for many years. The idea that she is Vlad's wife reborn was hard to believe. He knew he was the only one who could translate the message though. Still surprised, David translated, "He just said there is a painting of Prince Vlad Dracul's wife. He lost to tragedy and has been searching for her soul to be reborn in a new body ever since. The person who

DRACULA

entered the room last, looks like the one in the painting."

When everyone heard David's translation, they were all in shock. Donna seemed to be in shock more than anyone else. While she was in shock, Donna asked, "Me?! What do you mean?!" She continued as she said, "There is no way I am Dracula's lost love." She then thought of another question and asked, "If I am Dracula's wife from a long time ago, why would he want to put me through hell like we've gone through since we got here?!"

Frank threw out an answer without really thinking if feelings would get hurt, or if it would simply bother a member of their group without actually hurting their feelings. He answered, "Duh, as if it wasn't obvious. Dracula wanted to bring you here to get you back. When he realized you had a beau, he had to get rid of the competition."

Donna listened to every word and she believed that it made some sense since Dracula's first victim was her beau she came to the castle with, Arnold. While thoughts raced through Donnas' mind, Janice decided to act on Donnas' behalf. She asked with a mean look on her face and an angry tone in her voice, "How would you feel if roles were reversed and Dracula killed me?!

DRACULA

What if you were his target to torment?"

After Janice made Frank think about what he said, Frank responded, "Man, I wish I could rewind time and take back what I said."

Janice was not interested in hearing Frank's apology though. She acted as though her ears were plugged and she could not hear. In actuality she could hear just fine but her mind was clouded with rage. Mad as she was, Janice ignored what Frank was saying and stomped her way out the door and into the hallway.

Once in the hallway, she looked down the hallway as she was preparing to go for a short walk to cool her temper down. As she looked down the hallway, she saw ghosts in the hallway about halfway down from David's assigned bedroom. They were two ghosts standing in the middle of the hallway a few feet apart from each other. They were dressed as court jesters. The fools were practicing their juggling act. The jester ghost facing toward David's assigned bedroom saw Janice as she came out. The fool thought that it would be nice to have an audience after centuries of practice.

Janice had her own thoughts about what she saw. She was not interested in watching ghosts juggle. She said with nobody else

DRACULA

there to listen, "This place is infested with more ghosts than I thought." Her heart was racing as she hoped the ghosts would not try to juggle her, or throw their things at her. Fear of what could be took the place of the anger she felt when she left the room. She slowly reopened the bedroom door and went back inside. Before anybody could ask her why she left the room, or why she came back she said, "There are ghosts in the hallway."

DRACULA

Chapter 18

New Ghosts Found

Frank was surprised to hear there were more ghosts to contend with, as were the others. Frank though was the one whose arms Janice ran into when re-entering the room. He said to Janice, "Everything's okay." He paused for just a second then continued; "Tell me," he asked, "What were these ghosts like?"

Janice took a breath and then did her best to describe these new ghosts. She told her friends, "They didn't look dangerous, but you never know. They were *dressed like clowns and were juggling things that looked like one-thousand year old bowling pins." She could not help but to ask a question. She thought it would be taken as rhetorical, yet at the same time, hoped for an answer in the back of her mind. She asked to nobody in particular, "What if they got violent and decided to throw those things at us?"*

Everyone was not sure what to think. Questions popped into everyone's minds. Most of which were questions nobody dared to ask, being afraid of possible answers. Alicia tried to give words of comfort even though she was scared to hear new ghosts were abroad. She said, trying to calm down Janice, "It's alright. You are in here with us, while they are out there."

Janice became very scared as she felt the castle was filling with even more ghosts. She became overwhelmed with the feeling of being boxed in. Her overwhelming feeling caused her to say, "Oh, no. I have to use the bathroom."

Frank replied, "You're my girlfriend. I will take you there so you don't have to face these new ghosts alone."

David then said, "We will wait here for you two to return." After a second of silence, David said, "Be safe."

DRACULA

Frank replied to David's concern, "Thanks." He then turned his attention to Janice and put his hand out. He then said, "Take my hand. I will walk you to the bathroom."

Janice was flattered that her beau would face these new ghosts with her. She was still scared at the same time. In an attempt to relieve some of her fear she took Frank up on his offer and grabbed his hand. Janice then said, "Let's go."

Just as they were getting ready to leave the room, the soldier ghost that David has been talking to said in Romanian, "Be careful. More ghosts may impede your path."

DRACULA

Frank asked, "What did he say?"

David responded, "He said be careful. More ghosts may impede your path"

Frank responded, "Okay, thanks for the tip." Frank and Janice then left the room. Once in the hallway Frank said, "Come on. I will walk with you to the Bathroom door."

Holding hands and beginning to walk down the hallway to the bathroom door with her beau, Janice said, "Thank you. I don't know if I could have done this without you."

As they walked to the bathroom, they past the juggling ghosts. Neither of the ghosts seemed to pay any attention to Frank or Janice as they walked by. Frank began to feel like Janice's personal hero. He felt as though he protected her all the way to the bathroom from David's assigned bedroom. Feeling a rush of bravery, he decided to make a bold move before letting go of Janice's hand. He pulled her in close and gave her a kiss. As soon as the kiss ended, Frank said to Janice, "I'll wait here just outside the door for you."

With her heart racing from the kiss, Janice responded, "Okay. I'll be right out."

Janice went into the bathroom, and Frank stayed just outside the door and felt like a security guard protecting his prize possession, his girlfriend. Keeping a look out for anything dangerous, Frank centered most of his attention on the juggling ghosts. He was in awe as he noticed the items they were juggling seemed to change shape like magic.

Right before his eyes, what looked like bowling pins being juggled turned into knifes being juggled. As the change took place in front of his eyes, Frank dropped his jaw and said, "What the?!" Frank's shock was so great; he was unable to finish what he wanted to say. Frank became scared, not knowing what would happen next. He did his best to mask his feelings by watching the juggling show with great interest.

Meanwhile, back in David's assigned bedroom concern was growing. Donna asked, "If they get separated, one inside the bathroom, the other outside, doesn't that make them both easy prey?"

Alicia, having the same concerns and feminine instincts replied, "You're right. They may be easier to pick off separately. I hope they're both okay."

David decided to get in on the chat with his thoughts. He said, "You know, in most fight movies I watch they use a tactic called divide and conquer."

DRACULA

Unknown to all, this is what was happening in the bathroom. Just as Janice was getting ready to use the bathroom, Dracula materialized directly behind her. He then sank his fangs into her neck. Before she knew it her blood was being drained at a rapid rate. The lack of blood made her feel cold.

Soon, so much blood had been lost that she passed out. He then let go of her neck with his vicious bite grip. Dracula then dragged Janice by the back wall of the bathroom. He then grabbed a hook from the back wall and pulled. All of a sudden a passage opened in the back wall. Dracula then dragged Janice through the opening. It stayed open for only one minute then closed on its own. Dracula used the secret passage to transport Janice's body to the tower.

Meanwhile, not knowing anything has happened, Frank remained outside the door standing guard. Frank's concern began to rise as he noticed Janice was not coming back out. He said thoughts aloud as he was waiting, "I hope she's okay."

At the same time, tension was building in David's assigned bedroom. Donnas' tension was building in the room more than any of the others. David and Alicia were worried too, but Donna could not stand there and wait

DRACULA

any longer. Donna decided to shout, "I can't stand waiting anymore!" She continued as she said, "I have to see if Frank and Janice are okay."

Donna then went running out the door. As she was leaving, Alicia said, "Be safe."

As Donna left the room, she saw for herself what was going on. She saw two ghosts in the hallway juggling blades. She saw Frank waiting at the bathroom door. With fear in her eyes, she walked past the two juggling ghosts. Once past them, she turned her walking into running. She wrapped her arms around Frank once she was close enough feeling overwhelmed

DRACULA

with joy seeing that he was still safe.

Frank was caught off guard. He did not expect to see Donna out in the hallway. He especially did not expect that Donna would run into his arms like she did. Frank, not knowing what was going on said, "Thank you for the hug." He then asked, "But I can't help but ask what you are doing out here in the first place?"

Donna found herself on the spot to explain her actions. Not wanting to lie to Frank, someone she had been friends with for years she explained, "I thought you and Janice were taking a bit too long. I decided to see for myself if you two were okay still." She ended

DRACULA

her thoughts by asking, "I can see you are okay, but is Janice?"

Frank had no answer for Donnas' question. All he could say was, "I'm not sure. Let's find out."

DRACULA

Chapter 19

Regroup

Together, Frank and Donna went into the bathroom in order to investigate what was taking Janice so long. Donna opened the door and took a look first, one female to another. She noticed immediately that the bathroom was empty. She said, "Frank, look!"

Frank agreed to take a look immediately since Donna sounded surprised. He was curious what it was that surprised Donna. As he went to take a look he asked, "What's wrong?"

DRACULA

Donna had no answer for Frank's question. Donna had no clue what to say to Frank as he began to take a look.

Hearing no response, but seeing what Donna saw told him everything. The room was empty and there was only one door to the room that they knew of. Frank could not help but ask another question. This time the question was rhetorical. Saying thoughts aloud, Frank asked, "Where did Janice go?" Frank does not know in his gut, that Donna, nor, any of his other friends could answer his question.

Donna responded, "Come on. We need to let the others know

what is going on. Let's get back to the others."

As they were returning back to David's assigned bedroom cautiously as they passed the dagger juggling ghosts. As they got near the ghosts, their juggling act changed yet again. Dagger by dagger as they were tossed in the air they changed shape. The blades left the ghosts hands as daggers, and they change shape into full size swords.

The swords were caught as they came back down. The design of both the daggers and the swords were from hundreds of years ago. They were of the same designs used back in the fifteenth century.

DRACULA

That is the same century as when Vlad Dracul lived.

Donna and Frank watched in amazement as they saw different things getting juggled. At the same time fear of having a sword thrown at them lurked in their minds. They did not stay to watch, but kept a good eye on the juggling ghosts as they walked by. It did not take long to get back to the door of David's assigned bedroom.

They opened the door and as they stepped in Alicia asked with a concerned look, "What happened?"

Frank felt that he should answer. He gulped then replied, "Well, I walked Janice to the bathroom door. She went in; I

DRACULA

stayed just outside the door like a guard, keeping an eye on the hallway ghosts. Next thing I know Donna is coming down to check on us and Janice is not coming out."

Sounding like a person wanting to solve a puzzle, David responded, "If you were guarding the door, and when looking inside Janice was nowhere to be found, than that must mean that a secret entrance is involved." He continued his thoughts aloud, "The question is, did she find the secret door and go exploring? Or, did someone find her and snatch her, taking her through the secret door?"

Alicia entered the conversation by expressing her own

thoughts, "Well, I for one don't think she would have gone through any secret doors by choice. She knows how we are all scared. I thing she was taken, and perhaps killed like the others. It seems to me, no room in this castle is safe. Now that we are dealing with ghosts in the hallway now too, it seems that walking room to room is no longer safe either."

"Agreed," said Frank.

Donna then asked, "What do we do now?"

The soldier ghost in David's assigned bedroom decided to give information by saying, "Ascultă-mă pe toate. Acest castel este blestemat. Singura modalitate de va fi sigur este dacă este ridicat blestemul."Donna asked, "What did he just say?"

David replied, "He just said, listen to me all. This castle is cursed. The only way you will be safe is if the curse is lifted."

Frank then asked, "How can we lift the curse of the castle?"

David replied, "I'll ask." He then repeated the question in Romanian, "Cum putem ridica blestemul castelului?"

The soldier ghost in David's assigned bedroom replied in Romanian, "Care este necunoscut pentru mine. Eu nu sunt sigur că oricine are aceste cunoștin☐e."

Knowing that translation is needed, David translated immediately, "He said, that is

DRACULA

unknown to me. I am not certain that anyone has such knowledge."

Frank then said, "Damn. It sounds like this is one puzzle that still needs to be solved. We are running out of both time and help with our friends missing."

Attempting to be the voice of comfort Alicia said, "We may be running out of time, but we are not out of time. There has to be a way to lift this curse just like any other." She paused a moment as she thought. As an example entered her head she said, "You know, there was a voodoo man in a Scooby-Doo story. He protected himself by sacrificing a chicken."

DRACULA

Frank replied, "Hey I remember that one. Too bad we don't have a chicken to sacrifice."

Donna then replied, "You know, I saw an article online recently about curses. It basically said that you need to give off positive vibrations to break a curse on you."

David then replied, "Yeah, but the curse seems to be on all the ghosts in the castle, not us."

Donna then said, "Okay, now I'm confused." She continued as she asked, "How is a ghost supposed to give off vibrations, positive or negative? Don't they need bodies in order to give off vibrations?"

DRACULA

Chapter 20

Betrayal or Sacrifice

As the debate continues in David's assigned bedroom, Dracula was in the tower planning his next move. Thinking aloud he asked to nobody at all really, "Who should I kill next?" At the same time he rubbed his hands together in anticipation.

His body then dematerialized as he hunted for the castle's guests, hoping to find them in separate rooms. One eye rematerialized in the common room, the other in the dining room. To Dracula's dismay, both rooms were empty of the guests.

Finding no one in either room, he made both eyes dematerialize once again. This time he made one eye rematerialize in the bathroom, the other in the pantry. Still all he came upon was empty rooms.

Dracula knew that if those four rooms were empty, than they must be in the bedrooms somewhere. He then decided he did not want to search through every room connected to this hallway. Dracula knew that they had to come out sooner or later. They could not stay in the bedrooms indefinitely. If for no other reason, their bladder would get the best of them, sending them down to the bathroom.

As Dracula lay in wait, he kept himself amused as he watched the ghost jugglers perform their juggling act. As for the four friends feeling trapped and cornered, panic began to slowly set in. Knowing now the reason they were accepted to go on this trip put everyone on edge. None of them could help but wonder who Dracula's next victim would be, or if simply hiding in this room would somehow keep them safe.

As the chat continued, they became both confused and scared. Donna, trying to get everything straightened out in her mind asked, "Okay, if curses have to do

DRACULA

with negative vibrations, and ghosts have no bodies to give off vibrations, than how is this curse over this castle still happening?" She paused, but only for a second. Before anyone had a chance to answer she came up with yet another question. She asked, "And how am I supposed to be Dracula's lost love?" She continued by saying, "All I know about him is what I've seen in the movies. I have no feelings for tall, dark and fangy."

Frank then said, "Time out, new topic. I am having blood sugar issues. I need to get a snack." He then asked, "Does anyone else need anything?"

DRACULA

David then said, "Okay, let's make a plan. Frank, since you are hungry, and Dracula seems to favor Donna, you two should go together to the pantry. So far, this room seems to be pretty safe. Alicia and I will wait here for you two to return with the snacks." David then asked, "How does that sound?"

Frank responded, "It sounds like a plan to me. You two stay safe here, while we stay safe together as we get the food."

David gave Frank two thumbs up and said, "Ok."

With that, Donna and Frank headed toward the door. Being a gentleman, Frank opened the door and said, "After you."

DRACULA

Donna, wanting to be lady-like in return did a curtsy, although she was not in a dress and said, "Why thank you sir." Donna then left the room first before Frank. The first sight seen by Dracula as he continued to spy was Donna, the reincarnation of his lost love.

Dracula saw his once beloved and hoped she remembered their everlasting love from ages ago. He then saw Frank as he followed behind Donna out of the room. Seeing the two together, Dracula assumed that Frank was Donnas' new love. Going on the assumption that he was correct Dracula had only one thing on his mind. He thought to himself, "I must free her from him now. She must realize that I am her one true love."

The idea that his love from ages ago could love three different men in one night he found to be outrageous. The thought that she could love any man in sight that seemed available seemed to be too much to comprehend. Dracula's heart seemed to tear in four directions. Wanting all of the love his love from the past had to give, his heart stretched out to her, as well as the three men she shared her love with tonight.

Dracula felt both pain and anguish. His emotions finally came to surface after being submerged in the deepest, darkest places in both

DRACULA

his being and his castle for hundreds of years. The feeling of a flood of emotions that have been kept hidden for hundreds of years felt overwhelming to the prince of darkness.

As Dracula was dealing with his emotional state, Donna and Frank continued to the pantry. They did not notice Dracula's eyes spying on them at the end of the hallway. Once again, Frank being a gentleman opened the door to the pantry. He opened the door with his right hand, and with his left he waved it across his body as he said, "Ladies first."

Although neither Frank nor Donna could notice the flux of emotions flowing through the

DRACULA

castle, all the castle ghosts could. This too went unnoticed by Frank and Donna.

Donna entered the room first, accepting the polite invitation on Frank. Frank then followed, closing the door after entering. Donna and Frank began to look through the pantry. Donna was talking as she was looking, "Let's see what we got here." She paused a moment then said, "None of these labels are in English." Still saying her thoughts aloud as she was looking, she asked herself, "How are we supposed to know what there is to eat?"

Overhearing her thoughts aloud, Frank decided to answer the question asked by Donna, "The

DRACULA

only way I can tell is if we look at the pictures on the boxes. At least that will give us a clue as to what's inside."

With Donna thinking she was safe because she was believed to be Dracula's love reborn, and Frank thinking he was safe since he was accompanied by Donna, neither one kept their guard up in the pantry. Unknown to them both, they were not alone. They believed that the only thing in the room with them was the food kept in the pantry. As they both had their faces buried in the pantry in an attempt to figure out what there was to eat, Dracula began to materialize behind an unaware Frank.

DRACULA

All of the sudden, Donna turned around. She was about to ask Frank, "Have you found anything?" Instead, her voice seemed to be mute as she saw Dracula materializing behind Frank. She wanted to warn him, but no words seemed to want to come out. Donna decided that if she could not help verbally, she would attempt to help physically. She ran over to Frank as Dracula was zeroing in on his target.

Dracula's mouth watered as the thought of getting rid of his competition ran through his mind yet again. As he lunged in to get Frank, Donna beat him to Frank. Frank had no clue as to what was going on. All he knew was that he was pushed. By who or why he was currently unsure.

Dracula never planned on being interceded, least of all by Donna. With momentum carrying toward Frank's position, now occupied by Donna, and the thirst for more blood being the only thing on his mind, Dracula ended up sinking his fangs into the one he tried not to bite, Donna. Once his fangs entered Donnas' neck, Dracula's thirst for blood kept him from releasing his grip.

As Frank stumbled and reclaimed his balance, he turned around to see the blood, and the life, both slowly being drained in Donnas' eyes. As he saw what was going on, emotions and thoughts ran rapid through Frank's mind and body. He seemed to be frozen as he watched. Was it concern he felt most for the loss of a dying friend during her last moments that pondered in his mind as he remained frozen?

Was it amazement to see that so many ghosts are not only real, but that they could be so deadly? Was it fear seeing the life being drained from Donna and wondering if he was next? Was it simply confusion, wondering still, why he was pushed?

All these thoughts and emotions plus many more overwhelmed Frank to the point to where his body and mind remained frozen as he tried to straighten out a huge mess within his head.

Dracula, unable to prevent his thirst for blood from getting the better of him took little time to drink all the blood from what was once Donnas' body. Once finished, anger set in to Dracula's mind; anger from Frank avoiding his attack, and anger from Donna blocking the attack. Dracula decided to release his anger, release it on none other than his intended victim, Frank.

With an angry face, and blood dripping from his face, Dracula lunged in, going straight for Frank's neck. Frank stayed where he was, frozen. Some would have guessed frozen in shock, while others may have guessed frozen in fear. No matter what it was that was keeping him frozen, the result remained the same. Frank was a man who found himself unable to move. He was a man unable to mount either an offense or defense. Before Frank was able to act or react, he found himself of the wrong end of a blood draining exercise.

Dracula acted fast. He had emotions ranging from high to low and everywhere in between. He wanted to kill Frank in an instant, but even Dracula could not drink that much blood in that short of time span. He drank Frank's blood though the fastest, and with more force than the prior victims of the

DRACULA

night. Frank lost his blood in half the time it took Dracula to drain Donnas' blood. In no time at all, Dracula stopped drinking Frank's blood, and Frank fell to the floor, a blood empty shell of his former self.

With the blood from both Frank and Donna in him, he felt super strong, as though he had twice the strength because he had twice the feeding. With this enormous boost of energy, he picked up Frank, then Donna, each with ease. Dracula tossed each of them over a single shoulder. First Frank was tossed over his right shoulder. He followed suit with Donna, tossing her over his left shoulder.

DRACULA

Some ghosts wondered if there was any significance as to who was on which shoulder. Others did not give it even a single thought. Those who did though wondered; was Frank put over the right shoulder only due to Dracula being right handed and possibly had more strength on his right side. Others that questioned the significance wondered if Donna was over the right shoulder only due to the fact that the left side of the body is where the heart is kept.

Those who wondered knew of the lost love, and wondered if that was she. The others who gave it not one moment thought figured that Dracula wanted one for each shoulder and that was the way they were chosen to lay. Nothing special, just wanting to keep the weight evened out. Nobody knew for certain if there was some form of significance or not.

Holding them high upon his shoulders, Dracula opened a secret passage and carried them to his tower of collected corpses. It is a collection that has been building slowly but surely century after century. Not wanting to spend his time walking around, trying to find where the other two guests for the night were he decided to take a shortcut.

Dracula decided to once again to dematerialize himself. Once again, his body being the vessel to hold all that blood was gone, and the blood splashed to the floor of the tower. Uncertain where the last two were hiding, Dracula decided to try playing sly once again. At the end of the hallway he materialized each eye. The left eye in the left corner of the hallway, and the right eye in the right corner of the hallway. There, Dracula lay in wait, watching to see who is left, where they are, and where they are heading. Unknown to Dracula, the two who have avoided him so far had no intention of going into the hallway. Dracula was waiting and in the meantime, being amused by the ghost jugglers.

DRACULA

Chapter 21

Fear vs. Love

Unknown to Dracula, the two people he had yet to victimize had absolutely no intent of showing themselves to him. With thoughts of possibly dying, the only intent either David or Alicia had, was to stay hidden as best as they could. As they remained hidden within the boundaries of David's assigned bedroom, Alicia said, "So many of our friends have died tonight. They died before they were able to be loved completely by one another. I don't want that fate."

DRACULA

David understood what Alicia was talking about all too well, for he had similar thoughts race through his mind as well. David replied to Alicia as he asked, "I love you always, but do you really think that this is the correct place and time for sharing a special moment like that? I thought that was something special you wanted to share on our wedding night."

Alicia said, "That's true. I would rather wait for our wedding night, but with everyone dying, I don't think waiting 'til then is an option anymore. Now it is more like, I want to at least once before we die."

David replied, "I have to admit, I had some of the same

thoughts, but isn't that something you do during a time of passion? I don't think wondering if or when we will die tonight a time of passion."

Alicia thought he needed assurance that she was not asking for David to do this out of fear, but out of love. To prove her request was not based on fear, Alicia decided to grab David's right hand and lay it upon her left breast. She wanted David to feel her heartbeat. Once his hand was placed there she asked, "Does this feel like fear to you?" She continued as she said, "'Cause it's not fear in my heart. It is love for you."

DRACULA

Thoughts raced through David's mind. He couldn't believe that Alicia was so filled with love and passion instead of fear, considering their circumstances. David could not help, but to be impressed. He began to draw strength from the passion and love he felt coming from Alicia. Passion and love was taking the place of fear inside of him. Fear and doubt for survival left his mind as he kept his hand where Alicia rested it upon her breast and he came closer. He felt her heartbeats pace fastened as he came closer. He brought his lips to hers and together they shared a kiss of passion.

DRACULA

As passion filled the room, the ghost soldier felt out of sorts. He knew he was cursed to wander the castle until which time the curse would be lifted, which seemed to him would be never. At the same time, he felt he was imposing on the young lovebirds first moment of true togetherness. Feeling his conflict of interest, he decided the only true way to resolve his conflict, and let the prize winning couple have their special moment to turn his back from any and all action going on in the bed.

Body temperature was rising between David and Alicia as they began to feel more than warm from the kiss. For each of them, it felt like their hearts were moving faster than ever. Besides making them both feel all warm inside, the kiss also made Alicia weak in the knees. She sat on the bed, not letting her eyes off of David. David did not let his eyes off Alicia either. David did not realize though, that the reason she sat was because she was weak in the knees. He simply thought it was the next stage of development, going from a standing passionate kiss, to actions of sitting down or lying down on the bed.

With their eyes staying connected, David sat next to Alicia. Alicia began to unbutton her blouse which was purple. It was easy for David to figure out what she had

DRACULA

in mind. David decided to mirror Alicia's actions in a way. Since she was disrobing her shirt, he would do the same. David of course was wearing a different type of shirt. Being a sports fan from Michigan, he was wearing a Detroit Tigers jersey. He began to unbutton only seconds after Alicia. They finished unbuttoning their shirts at almost the same time.

David noticed instantly that as Alicia was unbuttoning her bra seemed to be different from the ones he has seen in commercials. The ones being remembered from commercials were white with no design. The bra Alicia was wearing though was different in more than one way. Alicia's bra was red, and

DRACULA

it had a flower design on it. In areas where there were no flowers, the bra was see-through. It was hard for David not to stare.

Alicia took notice of his staring, as she too was staring, at his chest. Although Alicia wanted to act upon the impulse of seeing more, she put her hands upon his chest and slowly moved her hands from the middle of David's chest up to the shoulder. As she moved her hands across his chest, his open shirt followed the same path. Her plan was executed to perfection as David's shirt began to slide off his shoulders. Now Alicia could see even more. She could see David's muscles as they slowly became revealed.

DRACULA

Alicia was pleased with her plan thus far. She felt David's muscular biceps and liked what she both saw and felt. As she felt up his muscles she said, "Those are some nice, big muscles. I hope to find more."

David grinned. He decided that since Alicia took the initiative to remove his shirt, he would be next to take initiative to see more. David leaned in for a kiss. While giving Alicia a French kiss, he brought his hands to her breasts. From there, David slid his hands up to Alicia's shoulders, sliding her shirt off her back.

The feeling of David's hands against her breasts enhanced the feeling of escalating hormones in

DRACULA

Alicia. It made her want an even deeper and more passionate kiss. As Alicia felt her shirt slide down off her back, she waited only a second for the shirt to slide off the rest of the way. She then brought her arms up behind her back and unclasped the bra.

All of the sudden, David noticed the bra straps next to his hands were quite loose now. He slid his arms down from Alicia's shoulders to his wrists. The bra followed to the wrists and beyond, falling off Alicia and on to the floor between them.

With both of their top halves completely bare, it was time to make the next move and work on making their bottom halves bare.

DRACULA

With his hands down by their waists, David took it upon himself to make the next move. He grabbed at his belt and quickly unbuckled his belt. At the same time he was moving his feet. As he finished unbuckling his belt, David kicked off his shoes.

Alicia noticed how he was multitasking. Thinking David either needed or wanted help, but was unable to ask with his mouth being preoccupied Alicia went to unbuckle and unzip David's pants. Wasting no time, Alicia pulled down David's pants. With her hands as low as they were, she hurried and took her shoes off.

As Alicia stood back up, David decided he wanted to return

DRACULA

the favor. He felt her breasts as she stood back up, followed by her stomach and hips. His hands ended up at Alicia's belt buckle. Returning the favor, David unzipped Alicia's pants and slid them down her legs. They were recently shaven and felt as smooth as silk. As he slid the pants down, he came across another surprise. It was not as much as a surprise though as the sexy bra. This surprise was the fact that Alicia was wearing a matching pair of underwear.

David always saw the white pairs worn in commercials. David figured that if her bra was not the standard commercial design, then why should her underwear be?

DRACULA

David was able to see through sections of Alicia's underwear, and he liked what he saw. The same as he liked what he saw and later felt with her breasts. David's hormones were raging already as were Alicia's.

Alicia decided that it was time to climb in the bed and get busy doing something other than stripping clothes off one another. She yanked back the comforter and slid under the top sheet. David thought the way Alicia climbed into bed was sexy. He then climbed in after her. The one thing he refused to do after everything that has happened tonight was leave his girlfriend alone in bed, almost completely nude.

They were where they wanted to be, at the time they wanted. Nothing was going to stop them from enjoying complete joy and satisfaction. David climbed into bed after her. Once under the sheet, David went to lay his hand upon Alicia's waist. David thought that what he would find was her underwear that still needed to be removed. Instead, David found himself in unfamiliar territory. His hand landed in an opening. It was Alicia's vagina. David was not intending to give Alicia a finger job though.

David felt Alicia's hands upon his waist line. She was feeling for

DRACULA

his underwear. Once she found the elastic strap at the top, Alicia began to wiggle David's underwear off. They were finally able to get down to business. With the last bit of clothing now out of the way, they moved in even closer. They kissed as they moved closer together. When they got close enough, nature took its course. It was like a key fitting into a lock with perfection.

Body heat began to rise to the point both bodies were feeling like furnaces. Hormones felt like exploding like a volcanic eruption. For the first time in both David's life and Alicia's life, full satisfaction was reached, and virginities were traded.

DRACULA

All the while, the ghost soldier in David's assigned bedroom kept his back to the action. The ghost soldier felt awkward being in the position he found himself. He did not want to leave the room he had been haunting all these years, at the same time, he did not have the personality of a peeping tom. He listened for the sound of silence, the sound of moans ended.

When the two young lovers were done, and they both felt exhausted as well as relieved, they each gave a sigh of relief. All though the act of passion was done for the first time, they still had something to finish. They needed to clean themselves from the fluids they had just released.

DRACULA

Taking the under sheet with him, David saw a cleaning station against the wall. From it, he grabbed a handful of paper towel. David then made his way back to the bed to see to it that he and Alicia got cleaned off. Some of the fluids ended up on the bed itself, soaked through the sheet, some of it ended up on the top sheet. Some even dripped onto the floor as David went to get the paper towel. Last but not least, what missed the bed and floor was taken care of by the paper towel.

Even though David and Alicia each lost bodily fluid, neither lost the drive to act frisky. David and Alicia had the same idea. As they each grabbed a piece of paper

DRACULA

towel, Alicia reached down to clean off David's key, the only key to ever unlock Alicia's lock. David also reached down at the same time. His idea was to clean up the mess he helped create in Alicia's lock.

Knowing they were not yet dressed, the ghost soldier stayed where he was. He was waiting for them to finally get dressed and finish up. Was he waiting patiently though, or impatiently? Only he knew the answer.

David and Alicia were not yet done with their playing around. After wiping off one another's bodily fluids, they helped each other again. This time, they aided one another in getting redressed. They were now much more relaxed. Most of their tension has been released along with their bodily fluids.

DRACULA

Chapter 22

Ghosts Only Haunt At Night

Just as David and Alicia were trying to finish up with getting dressed, the ghost soldier turns around and sees that all they are missing with the process of completely getting redressed was their shirts. That however meant nothing to the ghost. Just as he noticed the progress or lack thereof on their part to redress themselves in a timely manner, they too noticed something about the ghost.

DRACULA

As he turned around, he had an angry look on his face and his eyes were red. It was as though he was so angry; he had fire in his eyes.

Only seconds after turning around, the ghost spoke. In even less time, feeling an invasion of privacy, Alicia was quick to put her blouse on. The ghost said with anger in his voice, "Tu trebuie să vă grăbiți! Timpul este de esenta!"

David caught what was said right away by the ghost. Alicia on the other hand knew the ghost sounded angry but did not know the exact words. Worried that the ghost soldier was angry with them she asked, "What did he just say?

DRACULA

It wasn't anything horrible was it?"

David was surprised, both at the ghost soldier's anger, and Alicia's lack of understanding why he was angry. David decided that explaining things was the best thing he could do at the time. He said to Alicia, "The ghost said, you must hurry! Time is of the essence!" He paused only for a second and said, "As you have probably guessed, he said it with an angry voice."

Alicia was more confused than ever. She asked, "What does that mean? Time is of the essence? How is time going to save us from being next?"

David found himself without a way to explain. He was at a loss for words when it came to explaining the thoughts of the ghost soldier. Still, he knew an explanation was in order. David decided; if he was to explain everything to Alicia, he would first need some answers. David then said to the ghost soldier, "Ai atenția noastră. Ce înseamnă de timp este de esenta?"

Alicia quickly asked David, "What did you just say?"

David quickly replied, "I said, you have our attention. What do you mean by time is of the essence?"

Alicia then said, "Oh, good."

DRACULA

With the chatter coming to an end, the ghost soldier felt he could finally explain himself using Romanian. The ghost soldier said, "Aşa cum aţi observat, cele mai multe fantome aici nu sunt agresive. În curând, ca se apropie zorii nu va mai fi în compania aceste fantome. La răsărit, toate fantomele, dar unul se va odihni. Agitat fantoma este Duhul cel mai periculos care locuiesc pe acest castel, fantoma lui Prince Dracul. Dawn este la orizont. Se va odihni în curând. Aminte de avertizare meu."

All of a sudden, the ghost soldier vanished before their eyes. All the other ghosts disappeared as well throughout the castle. The disappearance of the others though was not seen by David, or Alicia.

David and Alicia both found themselves in awe. Alicia, though in awe was concerned about the final words of the ghost soldier. After seeing him disappear, she had to ask, "What did the bloody soldier ghost say to you before he vanished?"

David was still in awe. He knew that Alicia also wanted and deserved an answer. He said, "The ghost soldier was explaining everything to me. He said, as you have noticed, most ghosts here are not aggressive. Soon, as dawn approaches you will no longer be in the company of these ghosts. At sunrise, all ghosts but one will rest.

DRACULA

The restless ghost is the most dangerous ghost inhabiting this castle, the ghost of Prince Dracul. Dawn is on the horizon. I shall rest soon. Heed my warning."

Alicia began to say thoughts aloud, "All the ghosts are gone, all but Dracula."

David sighed then said, "Yes." He continued as he asked a question, a question that he was not certain if he wanted to be rhetorical or not. David asked, "Is having all the other ghosts gone a good thing, or a bad thing?"

Alicia was not certain if she should take the question as rhetorical or not either. Although the thought of the question being rhetorical ran through her mind, she felt she had to answer since there was no longer anyone else around who could. Alicia's answer was, "It must be a good thing. It means that there are however many less ghosts to have to deal with."

Relieved at the answer, and surprised to hear an answer at the same time David found himself with a strange look on his face. He thought to himself, "That question was rhetorical. Why did she answer it?" Those thoughts just remained to lay there in David's mind, as the only thing he is able to say aloud is, "Right."

Both David and Alicia knew the same thing. Although the ghost number has dramatically lowered, the one who remains between them and the path of victory is but one ghost, the most dangerous ghost of them all. They that knew they had the numbers advantage, two against one. They believed they had another advantage, the fact that they had solid bodies and their opponent is a ghost made up of ecto-plasma and was technically bodiless. With such advantages, what could go wrong?

With trying to pepping themselves up in courage, it began to build within them both. After thinking of their advantages, and not truly knowing their disadvantages David said, "Ok. It is dawn. We stayed the entire night; now let's find a way out of here."

DRACULA

Chapter 23

The Escape

Alicia shook her head in agreement as she said, "Agreed. We need to travel light and get out of here."

David used his left hand to open the door just slightly. At the same time in his right hand lay Alicia's left hand. With the door opened slightly, David peeked through the opening to see if there were any dangers in the hallway. He saw none. The hallway seemed to be completely vacated, not even the ghost jugglers were visible any more. With no dangers in sight, David said, "O.k., let's go."

They walked slowly out of the room, trying not to make a sound. They knew their friends were either missing or dead. These thoughts made David and Alicia extremely cautious. Whatever hurt or killed their friends they did not want to alert to their presence. Loud footsteps were out of the question in their minds.

Unknown to them, they just gave away their position. The one thing David failed to notice when he peeked through the hallway and Alicia failed to notice as well as they came out was Dracula's eyes at the end of the hallway spying

DRACULA

on them. It was an easy oversight though, for who looks for just eyes?

Meanwhile, six new ghosts arrived in the castle. They were Dracula's latest victims. The six new ghosts were spread out through the castle. They did not stay spread out for long. As ghosts, they had a sixth sense that they were just learning of. They were able to sense the presence of fear nearby. The six new ghosts rushed from where they were. In an instant they surrounded David and Alicia. All six ghosts interlocked their hands and made an ectoplasm box around David and Alicia.

The ectoplasm box surprised both David and Alicia. David was startled and jumped. He was shortly relieved when he began to take a closer look at whose ghosts they were.

Alicia's reaction was a bit different. Alicia decided that if she is going to be surrounded by ghosts she would scream, "Aaaaahhhhh!!!"

The scream had no effect on the ghosts, but it did hurt David's ears. He found it loud enough to pop ear drums. David was lucky in the fact his ear drums did not actually pop.

As soon as the ringing in the ears went away, David noticed that Alicia went from screaming, to panting. Alicia seemed to be hyperventilating. Calmly, and with a soft voice David said,

DRACULA

"There is nothing to be scared of. These ghosts are our friends who passed away tonight."

Scared still, Alicia latched onto David's arm and said, "They may be," and continued as she asked, "But what about the thing that turned them into ghosts? Do you think that is friendly?"

Such a thought scared David as well. It scared David well enough to make him gulp. It was the only sound in a long corridor. The gulp sounded loud, much like a lonely raindrop falling onto the ground in an ally off a rooftop.

Unseen before them, Dracula was wearing a sheepish grin as he was happy to notice fear coming from the two people he had not yet killed. Whispering under his breathe so nobody would notice, Dracula's eagerness and compulsion to get them all could not stop him from saying, "And there were two mice left in the cat's maze."

Alicia and David walked slowly as they were headed toward the end of the corridor. The ectoplasm spirits of their friends keeping the same pace. Cuffed together were the hands of the deceased friends as they surrounded Alicia and David. They too had their hands cuffed together as they faced whatever stood between them and the exit. The ghosts of the recently departed friends also spun around and around very fast. It seemed as

DRACULA

though Alicia and David were in a cyclone of ectoplasm.

From a distance, Dracula watched all. He found it amusing that Alicia and David were unknowingly walking straight toward him and what they did was hold hands one last time before deciding to go in for the kill. Dracula thought to himself, "What foolish lambs as they come to be eaten by the Dragon."

"Alicia," David said.

"Yes," Alicia responded.

David, continuing to hold Alicia's hand during their conversation said, "I want you to know, that no matter what happens; I will be right here at your side."

DRACULA

Alicia smiled knowing that David meant every word. He would be with her 'til the end. When David spoke, he said his message with a serious face, but seeing Alicia's smile made David smile. Looks of fear; worry or panic melted off their faces like snow on a hot summer day. Love, hope, companionship and togetherness now filled their eyes.

David and Alicia were now in a world of their own. A long corridor was no longer noticed as they looked into each other's eyes. Magic took its place as they saw visions of serendipity. The magic did not last long though as the constant reminder of reality stared them in the face, the reminder

DRACULA

was none other than aged castle walls that have stood for centuries with their torches burning bright.

As they entered back into reality, David and Alicia found themselves in the same situation as before. They were still surrounded by the ghosts of their fallen friends. They also still found themselves with most of a hallway to travel down. Being cautious David said, "Let's move slowly."

Alicia nodded her head in agreement and said, "Okay."

Although their plan was to move slow, which their feet were, at the same time it seemed as though their hearts were moving fast enough to run a marathon. As the cyclone of ghosts surrounded them, Alicia and David got half way through hallway, the eyes of Dracula, which had kept such a vigilant look out of the hallway, disappeared. This time it was only his eyes which he used to keep a look out with dematerialized.

In an instant, Dracula materialized on David's left. He attempted to charge the cyclone and get to the last two he had not killed. His first attempt was toward David. When the charging Dracula hit the cyclone he flew backward. This made Dracula think that the left side of the cyclone was strong. When Dracula hit the cyclone and flew back he also hit the floor. Dracula felt like running into the cyclone, then hit

DRACULA

the floor. It made him say, "Ooh, ah, ooh."

Dracula dematerialized yet again with haste. He then quickly rematerialized on Alicia's right. He decided he would take another crack at charging the cyclone, this time from the right side in hopes that the right side is weaker than the left. The effectiveness of the charges remained the same. Dracula flew back once again and said, "Ooh, ah, ooh."

As Dracula was working on finding the weak spot in the cyclone, the friends kept getting closer and closer to the exit. Dracula made another attempt to break through, this time his attempt came from behind.

Dracula hoped that the weak spot would also be their blind spot. Again, Dracula, much to his dismay was unable to penetrate the cyclone.

Thoughts of desperation to finish the killing job he began hours ago started to settle in after such a promising beginning. How to get past this ectoplasm force field spinning like a tornado seemed to be out of his minds reach. Attacking the cyclone from any angle did not seem to matter. Dracula was not even positive if his attacks were weakening the cyclone. The only thing Dracula was certain of was the fact that every attempt to get through thus far had failed. After his last attempt, Dracula decided to regroup by dematerializing once again.

The fact that he was dematerialized only put David and Alicia more on guard. This meant they had no clue where the next attack would come from. With thoughts of an ambush racing through both of their minds Alicia suggested quite instantly, "Let's hurry before he comes back!"

David said in an instant his reply, "I agree." With that, they went from a slow cautious walk, to a fast brisk walk.

Dracula sensed the urgency to act. Fear was no longer making them move slow like snails, fear now made them move fast like horses. With a sense of urgency to stop them, Dracula decided to make one final attempt as he stood rematerialized in front of the opened castle doorway. The cyclone was moving fast forward the doorway, with David and Alicia safely inside.

Dracula took the hit head on. The hit was strong enough to knock Dracula to the outside of the castle at sunrise. With the wind knocked out of him, Dracula did not think quickly enough. With the sun's rays hitting him he began to burn from head to toe, his entire body exposed to the sun. In a matter of seconds Dracula was burned out of existence here on Earth. All that was left behind was ash where he lay and met his demise. The ash did not remain there. It was a slightly windy morning and the ash was blown away, scattered by the wind.

DRACULA

Chapter 24

The Prize

With Dracula gone, the curse once held over the castle was now broken. All of the spirits once trapped in the castle could now move on. Alicia and David made it the rest of the way outside the castle and were able to see an amazing light show. Through the suns piercing light, the lights of the castle were seen as brightly as if the light show from castle happened at night.

The lights from the castle were no ordinary lights; they were spiritual orbs of light. They all

DRACULA

started in the middle of the sky. Some were blue and shot upward to the heavens. Others were red and were shot downwards into the pits of hell.

The spiritual orbs included all the ghosts trapped in the castle. Some were soldiers. Others were castle aids. Some were even those unlucky enough to take a dare and had not survived like those six friends who met their untimely doom in the castle and saved the last remaining two, David and Alicia through the use of a cyclone.

This left Alicia and David alone outside the castle with the Caretaker who arrived at sunrise. The Caretaker was there to see the light show of spirits being at long last released. Alicia and David noticed the Caretaker give a sigh. They believed it to be a sigh of relief without asking the Caretaker to confirm their suspicions.

The Caretaker after giving his sigh said, "Thank you, not just to the two of you, but your friends as well." The Caretaker paused a moment then continued, "Thanks to your group, the spirits have been released. That should mean that the curse over the castle has been lifted as well."

Alicia and David were both in shock. They did not even understand completely just what it was that they did to break the curse. Although they were confused on the matter, David responded as if he knew what was going on and said, "You're welcome. Glad to be of service."

The Caretaker then said, "You have both earned your ten-thousand dollar reward. I have decided to sweeten the pot though as some call it."

Hearing that made Alicia and David happy, yet at the same time they were sad for the loss of their friends. With a mix of emotions, curiosity fell into the mix. David, with his curiosity getting the better of him asked, "In what way do you mean?"

The Caretaker answered the question of curiosity as he said, "Well, as you know, we planned on ten people coming. That means we had one-hundred thousand dollars on standby in case all ten who we expected would have survived the night."

David and Alicia saw where the speech was headed and found themselves breath taken. At the same time, anticipation grew and they were tired from staying up all night. They both wanted to go home now and get some sleep. Thoughts of interrupting the Caretakers speech ran through both of their minds; however they both thought it would be rude knowing the manners they were taught.

With no interruptions, the Caretaker continued, "I saw the results of your visit. Many, if not all the spirits trapped here have finally been able to move on. As thanks for finding a way to set free many trapped souls from hundreds of years of confinement I issue you the sum of twelve-thousand, five-hundred dollars each."

They both were confused, Alicia, trying to take the confusion away asked, "How did the amount change if I may ask?"

The Caretaker assumed that such a question would occur. His assumption proved to be correct. The Caretaker explained, "The plan was to split one-hundred thousand dollars ten ways. Since only eight showed up, the money has now been split eight ways."

DRACULA

The Caretaker reached inside his coat and grabbed out two envelopes. With the envelopes in hand, the Caretaker continued as he explained what was in his hand, "In one of these envelopes is a set of eight, twelve-thousand, five-hundred dollar checks. In the other, you will find your airline tickets to return home. Take out the two checks with your names on them, and any two airline ticket sets of your choice."

The Caretaker paused for a moment to let David and Alicia a second to take in all of the information. He continued as he said, "I wish for both of you to rest assured that your friends will get a

DRACULA

proper burial paid for by the remainder of the money."

David and Alicia found themselves going from shocked to being breathless. The Caretaker handed the two envelopes over. The envelope containing the plane tickets was given to Alicia, while the envelope containing the checks was handed to David. Alicia was at a loss for words as she tried to comprehend what's happened over the past twenty-four hours. David on the other hand was able to find words while he was in shock, "Thank you sir."

Alicia sorted through the envelopes and found two for them with side-by-side seating. Alicia kept out the two she chose and put

DRACULA

the other eight back in the envelope. She then handed back the envelope to the Caretaker with the other eight plane tickets inside it. As she handed the envelope to the Caretaker Alicia said, "Thank you. Here is your envelope back with the other plane tickets."

As Alicia sorted and finished first, David sorted through the other envelope with the checks in it. David soon found the two with his and Alicia's names on them. David took those two checks out and placed the others back in the envelope. David said as he handed back the envelope, "Thank you. Here are the other checks you said you would use to pay for proper burials for our friends."

The Caretaker had a smile on his face and said, "Go now. Your taxi to the airport is a block that way." The Caretaker pointed into the direction of the taxi as he mentioned it. The Caretaker continued as he said, "The taxi driver has always been too cowardly to come all the way, but I guess you know that already from your drop off."

Alicia found the comment about the taxi driver funny. She then replied, "That sounds like him. Thank you and good-bye."

David and Alicia headed toward the taxi in the direction told to them by the Caretaker. Shortly after they began to leave, the Caretaker waved good-bye.

DRACULA

As they were headed toward the taxi, they too were headed into the sunrise. With the sun in their faces David said, "Home, here we come."

Alicia continued with her own thoughts vocally as she said, "When we get home, its college first, then we'll see."

With that, they walked a block going away from the castle. They took a short time to get back to the cab. The cab driver waited for them, standing in front of the cab. He had no plans to go any closer.

David and Alicia got back to the taxi. David was a gentleman and opened the door for Alicia. Once inside the taxi, David and

DRACULA

Alicia, the last couple remaining out of a group of eight sat next to one another as they headed back home. David put his arm around Alicia. In return, Alicia laid her head snuggly within David's arms where she felt safe from all harm.

The driver entered into the cab and began to drive. He took the young couple back to the airport. That is where they began the rest of their lives together.

Made in the USA
Middletown, DE
01 October 2015